Whispers In The Grass

International Intrigue - From the Montana Pastures to Pharmaceuticals: Horse Communication Cognitivity, and the Battle with Slaughter Houses

John F. Derr, RPh, FASCP, FHIMSS

The Reading Glass Books
1-888-420-3050
www.readingglassbooks.com
production@readingglassbooks.com

Dedication

This book is dedicated to my daughter Deborah Derr, DC the founder of United in Light Sanctuary to Save Draft Horses from Slaughter.

Whispers In The Grass is a work of fiction.

This is a fictional story about horses and the misconception that they don't communicate with each other, that their brains are the size of a walnut and they can only be trained to do minor tricks. It is about the new and emerging field of equine therapy and its use in medicine and a person's quality of life when they are ill or have a chronic condition with comorbidities. It is a fictional story of international espionage but based on a framework of facts. The characters are fictional and are not intended to represent anyone living or dead. The issues of slaughtering horses, Premarin Production, and horse meat consumption are true. Most of the information about geographic locations are true. The story is written in a sequence of 60 days during May and June of a year between 2025 and 2030.

Characters inspired by Crow, Blackfeet, and Zuni heritage (e.g., Son and Pelipa) are fictional and not intended to represent real individuals or communities. The novel honors these Nations' traditions, particularly their connections to horses and healing. Threats are fictional, from corporate entities, not tribal sources.

This book is drawn from my own life — places I've lived, people I've worked with, and landscapes I've come to know well: from the wind-cut waters of California and Anacortes, WA to the mountains of Montana, to long corridors of power in Washington, D.C. As well as the international countries of the world. In writing this story, I used emerging AI tools the way one might use a research assistant or editor — to help with grammar, refine phrasing, check historical detail, or spark structure. But every scene, every character, and every decision came from lived experience, memory, and the long craft of storytelling. This book is mine — rooted in the world I've seen, and the world I imagine.

Author Bio: John F. Derr, RPh, FASCP, FHIMSS, LTPAC Health IT Collaborative Emeritus. Graduate from Purdue University School of Pharmacy, Distinguished Alumnus in 2006. Executive Certificate of Business, Indiana Kelly School of Business (1970-71). After serving 5 years on Active US Navy on Destroyers he spent another 26 years in the Active Naval Reserve including 4 years as the Reserve Commanding Officer of two WWII Destroyers. He retired in 1989 as Captain, USN (1958-1989) and is the recipient of the Meritorious Service Medal. Derr has been a "C" level Healthcare Executive for over 60 years including: E.R. Squibb & Sons, Searle, Siemens Medical Systems, National Medical Enterprises (now Tenet), International Remote Imaging Systems (IRIS), Innovative Health Concepts (Metalaser), Kinamed Orthopedics' Implants (Kyocera), American Health Care Association/National Center Association for Assisted Living (AHCA/NCAL), Golden Living Senior Living Multi Group, Federal Advisory Committee for Digital Standards, Founder of the LTPAC Health IT Collaborative.

Introduction

It began, as many pharmaceutical discoveries do, with something barely noticed.

It had been five years since Jean Paul Kornig (JP) an ethnopharmacologist (Plant Pharmaceuticals) and Mariah Haynes president of James-Bandai Pharmaceutical Co Veterinary Division first worked side by side to develop a pharmaceutical cure for Alzheimer's from the bark of a Malaysian tree. The solution—and the question of who tried to steal it—took them from New York City to Japan and Singapore.

That trial forged more than a discovery. It forged a partnership—professional, personal, and enduring. What began in the shadows of *Ancient Cure* now led to new ventures, new questions, and new threats.

One phone call set the new course. Mandi's sister, Mariah, owner of Seneca Ranch outside Big Timber, Montana, reached out with startling news: a breakthrough study in horse–human communication using a revolutionary feed made from Montana Sweet Grass.

The implications were staggering. Such research threatened the global horse slaughter and feed- additive industries, igniting forces far beyond Montana's pastures.

Their story would begin in Anacortes, Washington… and end where the Sweet Water Grass™ stirred in the wind.

CHAPTER 1

Padilla Bay

JP returns to Anacortes, searching for rest and a place to begin again.

I eased my car into the gravel pullout at the end of Fifth Street and let the engine settle into silence. For a Moment, I just sat there with my hands loose on the wheel, listening to the soft hiss of wind lifting off the bay. The air smelled clean—salt on driftwood, kelp drying on rock, a faint resin of cedar from the hills. Underneath, there was that mineral hint from the refineries across the water. Even beauty came with infrastructure.

I stepped out and the world widened. Padilla Bay spread below in a sheet of dappled light, the low tide showing long bronze shadows where eelgrass patterned the shallows. Gulls angled and called in the cold blue. A ferry rumbled in the distance to the west, and far to the east Mount  Baker stood with its white cap catching every shred of sun.

At forty-three, the flights didn't forgive as quickly as they used to. Not so many years ago I trained my body to wake on the second beep of a watch alarm anywhere on earth. Now, after weeks on the road, the lag had to be worked out—walk it off, breathe it out, move your eyes across a horizon that doesn't bounce.

I took the footpath down. The house revealed itself in planes and lines the way good architecture does—nothing showy at first, then, detail by detail, your eye learns what it's seeing. From the water side it read as three tiers: a long, low garage at sea level for the Nordic Tug and the Cessna amphibious floatplane; a broad deck like a dock laid on pilings above it; and a clean two-story structure set back, the twin wing sections flanking a soaring glass great room. The second floor lived only in the wings; no structure sat over the great room to interrupt the sky. Inside, the ceiling climbed unbroken to the ridge, presenting a panoramic view.

I unlocked the side entry off the deck and stepped into the kitchen. The quiet held steady. I moved through the house by touch more than thought—palm along the polished marble counter, knuckles to turn a chair a few inches, fingertips on the cool steel of the fridge handle. I'd laid the plan like a field map: working triangles, clean sight lines, nowhere for clutter to colonize.

In the great room the glass wall faced northeast—Padilla Bay, the islands like low whales in the water, the sky a layered thing. Wide-plank fir floors kept their knots, not rustic so much as honest. Along the far wall, a built-in bookcase waited for the crates at my previous home in Los Angeles. A fireplace sat centered in local basalt, its lintel a slab salvaged from an old cannery.

I slid open the deck-great room door and stepped onto the deck. Two rocking chairs—hand- carved, high-backed, shaped to fit a human spine. They faced the bay a respectful distance apart. I let my hand rest along the back of one; the grain was rippled, luminous under oil. Danny Whulshad's work. Danny's granddaughter, Shana, had sent me an email weeks ago telling me that he had brought them by the week the windows went in. She texted that her Grandfather had told her to tie a welcome ribbon around each arm.

She added, "For sitting still. One for you, one for whoever you can stand long enough to share it with. Granddad carved the pair together. He said they don't like to be separated."

I answered her email by saying I'd do my best not to offend the chairs.

I sat now and felt the way the back caught me right where it should. The rocking found its rhythm after three short rocking passes, a slow pendulum that slid the weariness from my shoulders. Beyond the deck railing, the water colored itself from pewter to green and back again as a cloud moved across the sun.

I didn't turn on the deck music. I didn't turn on the great room television and I didn't check the news. The quiet had edges I wanted to think; you can't do that with noise in the house.

The kettle whistled and I moved back into the kitchen. I poured hot water over coffee grounds, breathed in the steam, and let memory surface in the order it wanted. The last flight was Tokyo to Seattle, the one before that was Singapore to Tokyo, the one before that a hop from a rural strip in Malaysia that didn't bother to be on most maps. I had come home with a fresh notebook of plant assays, three pages of political notes that would never live on a server, and a fatigue that felt less like weight and more like a film between myself and the rest of the world.

I moved from the kitchen back to the great room.

I'd asked myself once—back when I still wore my Navy uniform— whether I liked work or just felt responsible for it. The answer had stayed the same: both. Some problems don't use the front door. The best answers to those problems tend to grow from the ground up—quiet, patient, not flashy. I built a career going to where the answers lived and helping them survive contact with money and humanity.

Tires hissed on gravel and a truck door closed, muted by distance. Right on time. A text from ten minutes earlier still glowed on my phone: "Hardware samples in hand."

The front door opened and closed with a soft thud that carried down the hall. Footsteps, then Shana Lawrence stood at the edge of the great room, glove tips tucked in her back pocket, a rolled plan in her hand.

"Good to see you made it," she said. "Want me to note anything you want adjusted now that you're in the space?"

"Quality assurance begins with sitting still," I said, nodding toward the deck with a smile. "So far, the chairs pass."

She gave the view its due before unrolling the plan on the dining table and weighting the corners with four smooth beach stones that lived there for that purpose. "Walk me through any friction points. No rush."

"The banister is perfect. Stair rise is easy on the knees. Pantry shelves are exactly where my hands expect them. I'm still deciding if the island should be two inches closer to the sink."

"We can move it," she said. "Anchored, not welded to the earth." "You're going to tell me to live with it for a week and then decide." She nodded. "Also, Mandi will have an opinion."

"She will," I said. "She flies in tomorrow afternoon."

"Good," Shana said. "It's time she sees it in person and not by photographs." She made a small note on the plan. "Are you happy with house's livability?"

I considered the question instead of reaching for the polite answer. "Yes. It feels built to be lived in, not looked at. That's what I wanted."

Shana gave a single nod that read like respect. She set a narrow cedar box on the table. "Hardware samples for the deck doors. Stainless will do, but the blackened bronze will warm with hand oils and weather. Less glare in the morning."

"Let's see."

She opened it to a neat row of handles and latches on a felt bed, each with a small tag in careful block letters.

"You label like a field biologist," I said.

"My granddad made me catalog carving knives by steel and season," she said. "Do that for a year and you start labeling your socks."

"Tell Danny the chairs are earning their keep."

"I will. He'll remind you they were made as a conversational pair." She glanced toward the deck. "He says people talk better when they're facing the same horizon."

"They do," I said.

We walked up the upstairs and Shana made two pencil notes—one about a squeak on the fifth stair to the east wing, one about the way the afternoon sun might bloom through the clerestory in June. Back by the big glass we watched a tug push a barge south.

"Whidbey's been flying low this week," she said.

I heard them before she finished, the layered thunder of Navy jets pairing off above the clouds. I found them by ear and watched two rakes of contrail score toward the Strait.

"They sound like home to you?" she asked.

"They sound like freedom," I said. "And like a lot of people doing it well enough that the rest of us can drink coffee on a Tuesday."

She took that in. "My dad says almost the same thing. It is different coffee." "I still make my coffee like a Navy corpsman taught me in Sicily."

We stood quiet a moment more. The jets dwindled to a pale ribbon. She looked as if she were weighing a question.

"Go ahead," I said. "Ask it."

"Why a man like you builds a house like this, here, now."

"I wanted a place built for conversation and quiet," I said. "And a horizon I could trust." She nodded once. "Trust is something you can build. Helps to pick the right site."

We walked the exterior—the deck stairs to the boat level, the storage for lines and fenders, the wide openings that would swallow hull and floats without a scrape.

At the seaplane bay I measured the span with my eyes. Thirty-seven feet clear—after a fight with the engineer and a negotiation with the hillside. Approach angle, wind, tide, and the small honest judgment you make in your eye ball calculations.

"You'll want a heavier bumper on that southwest post before fall storms," Shana said. "I've seen logs come down the Bay the size of trucks."

"Noted. I may bring the Tug inside the first season and let the plane sit out while I learn the currents."

"Tell me before you try before a high tide," she said, dry. "I'll come take video on how much damage you do to the tug's pilot house."

I checked her face. She was teasing, a little.

We stepped into the utility room where the pump sat and the wash down hose was coiled in clean circles. The hum was low and even, the way it should be when a system is new and built without greed.

"You hear that?" she said, tilting her head. "Just the pump."

"And nothing else," she said. "No strain, no slap, no rattle. When you start to hear those, call me. Until then, you're good."

Back upstairs, I walked her to the door. The sky had shifted to that high Pacific Northwest overcast that looks gray until you notice how much light is in it. She pulled on her gloves.

"Mandi likes cedar?" she asked.

"She likes what lasts," I said. "And what's been cared for."

"Then she'll like this place. The home will ask for attention instead of drama." She paused. "I'll check lead times on the bronze door knobs and text you. Tomorrow—if you're out, I can drop a key for Mandi."

"I'll be here," I said. "There's nowhere else I'd rather be tomorrow."

When she was gone the house settled into its natural quiet. I moved to the deck and stood with both hands on the back of a deck chair. I watched a rain cell march by the far edge of the Bay. My eyes tracked its line and then it drifted unfocused, the way a person looks when he's not looking.

I've made a life of making sense of patterns that don't want to be seen. In the Navy, patterns lived in how people and things like ships moved in space and how they tried not to leave traces.

Later, in pharmaceutical manufacturing the patterns were in research and quality. Now my patterns were in plants and their alkaloids—and in the way humans hovered over live plants not realizing that all plants were a living part of the Earth's eco system. Researchers worked on extracting, naming, patenting, and forgetting where the knowledge started.

Somewhere else a cell phone might be ringing for me. I didn't want to borrow tomorrow's call today. I wanted to stand still long enough for this place to set a hand on my shoulder and say: stay.

I stayed. I sat. I let the chair move me an inch forward and an inch back until time itself took that rhythm. When I opened my eyes, the Bay had gone a shade darker and brighter, like two truths agreeing to share a frame. Mandi would be here tomorrow. When she stepped onto the deck and looked out, I planned to keep my mouth shut long enough for the place to say its name to her. If the future wanted to be planned, we could plan it from here.

CHAPTER 2

Arrivals

Recap: A new morning in Padilla Bay stirred memories and questions of what comes next.

Morning gathered slow and honest over the Bay. I stood on the deck with a coffee mug and let my eyes walk the water until they stopped trying to discover hidden areas. The tide had turned somewhere in the dark; you could tell by the way the eelgrass lay, combed one direction and then undecided in the backwash. A pair of gulls argued the merits of a piling. Somewhere far south a train placed itself along the shore one horn at a time.

Today, Mandi.

I cleaned without hustling. The kind you do with your hands instead of a list: fold the blanket over the back of the deck chair; square the books on the lower shelf; rinse the salt bloom from the windows and drag a chamois until the sky looked like itself again. I slid the island two inches toward the sink just to see if my knees noticed. They did. For the better.

Shana texted at 8:13: *"Bronze pulls confirmed. I'll leave the deck key in the cedar box. No need to wait around."* There was a period after every sentence. My favorite kind of punctuation.

I wrote back: *"Thanks. I'll be here. Pick-up is later this morning."*

Coffee. A shower. The quick check to make sure the bumper on the southwest post had enough padding on it for a stray log. Then the small, unglamorous things that make a house feel lived-in: the dish towel folded the way you like; the second mug left upside down so it's as clean as the first; the extra blanket in the basket by the door because people from New York always underestimate Pacific Northwest air.

At ten I drove into town and let the truck idle by the co-op while I bought bread that admitted it was bread—brown, seeded, and the right kind of heavy. I found early strawberries that had no business tasting like strawberries this far north and bought them anyway because the man behind the counter had good hands, and good hands don't lie about fruit.

On the way back I took the long turn by the marina to look at Cap Sante moorage I didn't need. Old habit: measure tide lines on pilings; see who keeps their lines coiled and who let's them snake; glance at the repairs nobody will do until the second storm. Routine is a language. Boats speak it. Be amazed at how many boats never get underway. Wave at the Alaska fishing boats getting ready to steam through the inside passage to the fishing grounds for halibut. Or put another way, just for the hell of it.

Back at the house, Shana had already been and gone. The cedar box sat on the table with a second, smaller key on a plain brass ring, "Mandi" taped neatly around it. A note under the lid in those block letters: *"Door weather-stripped; latch catch tuned. If it sticks, it's humidity, not you."* A single smile drawn in the corner. Not a grin. A diagram of a smile.

I set the key on the tray by the door and walked the rooms once more. When you expect someone you love, you don't decorate. You make space. The house already had the right kind of quiet.

At 9:30 I headed down the deck stairs to the seaplane and boat garage. With a click of the remote, the hangar door lifted. I settled into the cockpit, ran through the final checks, and eased the **Cessna Caravan Amphibian** into Padilla Bay. The Coast Guard had granted me clearance to operate there, and though seaplanes technically have right of way over pleasure craft, I always gave boaters extra room. Most weren't used to sharing the water with an amphibian.

The takeoff was clean, the bay falling away beneath me as the wings caught lift. Off my port side I glimpsed the worn outline of an old amphitheater, once a gathering place for Samish and Snohomish canoe races. Banking west, I crossed Guemes Channel—Anacortes off my left, Guemes Island to the right. Soon the familiar sprawl of NAS Whidbey filled the horizon, its runways and hangars a reminder of the Navy's constant presence.

The roar of jets stitched itself into the fabric of Anacortes life. Newcomers sometimes grumbled about the noise, but locals had a ready answer: *If you don't like it, move.*

Leveling out at 3,000 feet, I slid south along the coast. After checking in with Paine Field, I called Kenmore Air at Lake Union for clearance. At 10:30, the floats kissed the glassy surface of Lake Union, smooth as a sigh.

As I throttled back toward a mooring buoy, a figure on the dock lifted her arm. Mandi. She'd beaten me there.

The Zodiac came out to meet me, and moments later I was climbing onto the pier. She rushed forward, arms around me, her scent—familiar, intoxicating—sweeping me into a rush of memory and longing.

"You're early! I didn't expect you for another hour. If I'd known—"

"I couldn't wait," she said, smiling. "I wanted to surprise you."

"You did. I had lunch plans, but now I'd rather fly home and catch up."

"Perfect," she said. "Let's go."

Back in the air, we retraced the route north. Mandi leaned against the window, her eyes wide as Puget Sound opened beneath us, the Olympics rising to one side, the Cascades to the other.

As Anacortes came into view, I circled Cap Santé. "There's our house. Best view from up here."

She leaned closer. The home seemed cradled in the cliffside, framed by evergreens, the wing of the house wrapping around the soaring great room, the garage tucked neatly below.

"It's beautiful," she said softly. "Photos didn't do it justice."

"It's your design too," I reminded her. "You shaped it as much as I did. The only room you didn't touch was the great room. Wait until you see what Shana did with the interior."

I set the Cessna down smoothly, taxied back into the hangar, and closed the doors behind us. Together we climbed the stairs—first to the deck, then up again to the top-floor quarters—her luggage in tow, her presence already filling the space.

It was a slow welcoming kiss and hug. "JP, I know what you mean by catching up but I would really like to go to the deck and rest for a while and take in the view."

The bay did its slow work of making time feel wider. She sat and rocked once, twice, then let the chair decide the rhythm. Her eyes did the sweep: refinery tanks; shipping lanes; the long low back of the island; Baker in a white-on-white that never photographs the way it looks. Her hand found the blanket without looking.

"You built what you said you were going to build," she said.

"Shana and her Dad did," I said. "With your help, I wrote the requirements."

"Shana reads between the lines without inventing new ones," Mandi said, approving of a person with a competence that made her own life easier.

She tucked the blanket across her knees and looked at me over the rim of her coffee mug. "You good?"

"My answer is yes."

"Then we can begin," she said, and set the mug down. "Mariah called me."

Of course she had. You could feel a call like that coming across miles if you've lived long enough in the kind of work that makes calls like that necessary.

Mandi pulled out her cell phone and brought up three photos. The first was a barn post with an arrow sunk in it, the wood split to either side, the grain showing its surprise. The second and third were paper—cheap, ruled—the ink blocky and careful in the way people write when they don't want you to know how they hold a pen.

Stop the grass. Or be buried in it.

Livestock, not pets.

I felt the small narrowing behind my eyes that means my mind is already sorting, already discarding. I took the phone and pinched out to the edges. Splinters in the post suggested an impact angle below level—shot from a truck window or from someone shorter than the striking point. The handwriting was a performance in a block hand, but the left margin drifted inward, which meant the writer's natural habit was a right-tilting script they were trying to hide. The paper had been torn clean, then folded twice; I could see a faint crease where a thumb always learns to press.

"Two," I said.

"Two so far," she said. "She burned the notes. She was shaking when she told me and mad at herself after. She said she didn't want those words in her house."

"She's not wrong," I said. "She's also not wrong to tell you."

Mandi breathed out, not quite a sigh, more like a technician taking her hand off a switch after a good test. "She says the horses are doing something she can't explain in the Sweet Grass. She says Promise stands in it like he's listening to a long conversation."

"Promise is the foal," I said. "Molly Belle's son."

She nodded. "And she said—this is important—the grass has a scent. Sweet, not heavy. Vanilla."

"Noted," I said. A new note written next to an old staff line in my mind. "And she's getting pressure from the arrows?"

"Whispers, mostly. The written threats are the sharpest of it. But she says she's been watched. Headlights cutting slow by the gate at odd hours. A drone once. No plates she could read."

"Mariah doesn't spook," I said.

"No," Mandi said. "She doesn't." She rocked once more, thinking. "She asked me not to call the sheriff yet. Says the local deputy used to work on a Premarin Farm. He also visits the Canadian slaughterhouse to purchase edible horse meat and bring it back to the US. He drinks with the men who truck the Premarin mares out to the feeding lots when the Premarin Farm is done with them. I don't know if that's true. But she believes it."

"I believe her believing it," I said. "That matters for our timing." She looked at me over the rim again. "So what's our timing?"

I watched a ferry work across the edge of the bay like a white thought taking its time. The thing about timing is that it's always partly about respect. You go too fast and you break what you're trying to protect. You go too slow and someone else decides the pace for you.

"We can talk to her tonight," I said. "Video if she wants it, audio if she doesn't. We get her to walk the fence line with the phone, show us angles, show us where the arrows hit, show us what she sees when she turns her head. I want to know how close the county road is to that post."

"Half a field and a ditch," Mandi said. "But I want to hear her say it out loud." "She'll do it," Mandi said. "And then?"

"Then we make a plan to fly," I said. "If she's right about the pressure, it'll expand when she gets visitors to the Ranch,

"Tomorrow?"

"Let's talk about it tomorrow." I said, "Get caught up with a call tonight.

We were quiet long enough to hear the small smack of water under the deck. A tug worked a barge south. The jets on Whidbey held their noise for someone else's sky.

"You'll like the kitchen," I said, and watched her mouth tilt because it already liked the kitchen. "I like the deck," she said. "I like that it knows it's a deck and not a stage."

"That's Shana," I said. "She built things to be used." "Good," she said. "We'll use them."

We made simple food that always tastes more honest next to clean air—bread with butter that admitted its salt, strawberries that apologized for nothing, a salad you could name every leaf in. We ate at the small table because the view is for talking and today the talking was catching up since the last visit together in New York City 5 months ago..".

We let that sit where it wanted. Some sentences don't need a second sentence right away.

We talked in the way people talk who have worked together long enough to know which words earn their air. What we needed from her sister. What we didn't need from anyone else. What we would say if asked and what we would not say to anyone without a reason.

Back in the Great Room I showed her the cedar box. She turned the key in her fingers and set it back in its place.

"Good hand," she said of Shana's note.

"Good hands tend to know other good hands," I said.

She smiled at that—not broadly, not for show. The kind that is more like a small alignment of features than a declaration. I put the dishes in the sink and she walked the windows with a towel until they were overly dry. She was nervous as something was on her mind that had not come out yet. I said to myself, give the thought time, it will.

Late light. Not sunset, not yet. The kind of hour that makes the water lie about what color it is. We went back to the deck because you always circle back to the place where chairs do what chairs do.

She pulled her phone. "You ready?" "Ready."

She hit call

"Hey, it's me," Mandi said. "I'm with JP."

Mariah's voice came through small and steady, the way a person talks when she's measuring words for their ability to stand up in a field by themselves. "You two together is a relief I didn't know how to ask for," she said. "Do you have time?"

"We do," Mandi said. "Can you walk us through the situation?"

Mariah narrated what we couldn't yet see: the barn post; the notch in the rail where the second arrow had grazed; the ditch; the truck turn-outs you would pick if you wanted to shoot and drive. She stopped once and I heard horses in the near distance, the kind of low shifting sound a herd makes when it has somewhere to be but no hurry to get there.

"Promise is with them," she said, her voice changeable in a way that didn't bother naming itself. "He's been… attentive."

"Attentive is a good word," I said. "It makes you pay attention back."

She let a breath out like someone who'd been heard for the first time in a week. "I want to keep them safe," she said. "I don't know how to do that and keep the grass a secret at the same time."

"We don't have to do both forever," Mandi said. "Just long enough to understand what we're protecting."

"We'll talk about it when we get there." I said, "Maybe in a couple of days. We will call and let you know, okay.."

We ended the call with only the words required. Families say goodbye differently when there's work in the room.

Mandi slipped the phone back into her pocket.

We drew a line from here to there and marked it with nothing fancy. Then we put the map away because some lines don't like to be looked at too long before they're walked.

"JP, I am tired. It has been a long day." Mandi said without sounding tired at all.

I said, "Well isn't it time we visited the hot tub over there in the corner?"

"You are a sly man. You did not tell me there was a hot tub hidden on the deck. I can't think of anything better than to soak in the hot tub with a glass of wine. Are you up to it?"

"You bet I answered." I went on, "You just sit in your rocking chair and I will get us towels and a glass of wine."

I hoped out of my chair and walked over to the hot tub, turned up the heat, and removed the cover.

"I will be right back." I said excited at the upcoming event. Under my breath in just a little more than a whisper I said, "Now this is what I mean by catching up."

"I heard that JP." Mandi replied as she rocked her chair.

I think my race to the bedroom, then kitchen, and back to the hot tub was the speed of an eagle.

"Two towels, two robes, two wine glasses, a bottle of wine. and the glow of a western sunset hovering over the house. Just for us."

We disrobed in the dim light and slid into the tub. "What about the neighbors and the boats." whispered Mandi.

"What neighbors and what boats!" I said a loud. "This house was built for us and no one else."

CHAPTER 3

The Commitment

Recap: Old ties and new encounters hint at paths that will draw JP deeper into the story.

Scene 1 — Anacortes, WA — Morning, Next Day

Morning light filtered through the east-facing windows just after six. The sun had made its official appearance at 4:59, somewhere behind Mount Baker and the Northern Cascades, but the mountain range held the glow at bay until the sun could slip around the shoulders of the peaks. Gold crossed the floorboards, warmed the linens, and reached my eyes.

Mandi slept on her side, one arm tucked under the pillow, short auburn hair a loose compass around her face. The light touched her in delicate strokes, the kind a painter would spend all morning trying to earn. I let myself look. Five years, and the simple act of watching her wake still felt like being allowed into a private room.

I'd been with women before. None like Mandi. Beauty, quick mind, humor that cut through pretense, the kind of passion that shows up for work and for joy. And something I couldn't name that had first taken hold the day we met in James Pharmaceutical's Manhattan office—President and friend Phillip Bradshaw behind his wide desk, windows full of the city, and Mandi stepping into the room like an answer that hadn't yet heard the question.

Five years of distance since then: New York and the West Coast stitched together by holidays, consulting jobs, and escapes we saved for and planned like campaigns. It worked, mostly. Lately, though, I could feel it in her—quiet pressure collecting the way storm light gathers at the horizon. Marriage was on her mind. Was it on mine?

She stirred. Eyes opened slow, focus finding me.

"What are you looking at?" she said, voice edged with sleep.

"Nothing," I said, which made her smirk.

"How long were you watching me sleep?"

"You're imagining things."

She tossed a pillow. I caught it and sent it back. The wrestling turned to laughing, the laughing to kisses, and in the warm sweep of the morning light we made love again, unhurried, as if time had widened just for us.

We lay quiet afterward, breath easing, the window brightening by degrees. Somewhere below, a gull called from the rail as if making its case. A ferry sounded far off, more felt than heard.

I rolled out of bed and headed toward the shower.

"JP, let's talk—" she said softly behind me.

I paused and rapidly continued into the shower, "What did you say?"

"Nothing."

But I heard it. The words 'Let's talk.' sat there, small and heavy as an island.

Steam rose against the glass while the water found its temperature. I let it run over the back of my neck long enough to tell the body it lived here now, not in a plane or a hotel or a hallway outside a meeting room with people speaking in careful voices. When I came out she was sitting cross-legged on the bed in one of my shirts, hair towel-damp, watching the window. The gold had turned to white.

"Breakfast?" I said.

"On the deck," she said.

Scene 2 — A Conversation on Commitment

We took coffee and eggs outside. The bay lay calm enough to make the sky look like it had decided to lie down for a while. Sun glanced off the Bay; Baker kept its cap. I buttered toast; she stole half. We ate without ceremony, the way people do when the food isn't the point.

Mandi set her cup down and laced her fingers together, elbows on the table, eyes steady on mine. "JP, I've done a lot of thinking," she said. "Five years, six days, ten hours—give or take—and we're still calling what we have, a relationship. That's no longer acceptable to me."

I let the quiet be hers.

"I want commitment," she said. "Or at least a real plan."

"I don't disagree," I said. I leaned back in the chair as if to put the words where I could see them. "We have two choices. One: we get married. Two: we call it a beautiful five-year run and part ways."

She blinked, like the air had changed temperature. "So which is it for you?"

I hesitated, not for doubt but for the weight of saying it right. I shifted back, the chair caught a gap between deck boards, and tipped. I went over with a thud and an ungraceful flail of arms.

Mandi gasped, then saw I was fine and laughed, head back, the sound I'd fly three thousand miles to hear.

"Only my pride is wounded," I said from the boards. "But if you don't say 'marriage', my heart will be worse."

She slid off her chair and knelt beside me, hair falling forward. She kissed me once, quick. "Yes," she said. "Let's get married."

For a beat we did nothing but look at each other and breathe like we'd just come up from underwater. The future, which had been a hallway of doors, lined itself up into a single passage.

We sat there on the warm deck, back against the base of the table, letting the world go about its business—a tug pushing a barge south, a gull working the same patch of air, the faint hammering of someone framing a wall two houses over. The water glittered as if it had been waiting to be asked.

"Tell me when?" she said.

"As soon as we can do it right," I said. "Not fancy. Right."

She nodded. "Here?"

"Here," I said. "Or New York. Or both. But yes—here."

She took my hand and squeezed, then looked down at the chair as if deciding whether to forgive it. "We're keeping that story," she said.

"We are," I said.

She laughed again, softer this time, and leaned her head on my shoulder.

Padilla Bay held its light. Somewhere behind the hill, a neighbor's wind chime offered a few politely spaced notes. A small breeze carried the clean edge of salt, and the house seemed to rest with us, as if relieved we had finally said "marriage" out loud.

We didn't rush to make lists. We didn't call anyone. We just sat there long enough for yes to feel like it had found its home.

CHAPTER 4

The Letter from Montana

Recap: At Seneca Ranch, Mariah's draft horses and Sweet Grass whisper of change.

Scene 1 — Kayaking Plans

After breakfast, we were still a little giddy and decided to celebrate by keeping the day exactly as we'd planned it. The morning was bright and gentile wind—perfect for a paddle. I rolled the **Cessna Caravan Amphibian** out, ran the quick preflight, and we lifted from Padilla Bay, Baker riding off our left shoulder like a talisman.

Roche Harbor slid into view in its postcard colors. I set down long and taxied in easy. We grabbed a light lunch at the Hotel—fresh crab and bread that admitted it was bread—then walked to the outfitter. A tandem ocean kayak waited like a promise on sawhorses while we signed the form that says you know water has the last word.

Life jackets snug. Charts in a dry bag. Phones sealed. We slid off the float and let the first strokes find our rhythm: my draw, her sweep, the boat doing the math between us. The air held pine and salt and that faint sun-warmed creosote that tells you the day is fair. A bald eagle circled high and deliberate; a pair of harbor seals surfaced to second-guess our course and sank without offering advice.

With every stroke we moved together.

Scene 2 — The Bull Kelp Beds

We reached the kelp beds with the tide just right, the sea mottled with the dark disks of **bull kelp** bulbs and their long olive blades just under the surface. Sun threw coins of light that slid along the water as if someone were paying out a string of small debts.

I reached over, plucked a single kelp bulb, and put it to my lips. The bugle note carried across the water like a joke that got bigger in the telling. Mandi groaned and laughed at once, which is the correct review for a kelp-horn.

I bit the clean end of a blade and chewed. Tender, saline, a green crunch that tasted like the honest part of the ocean. "Clean ocean flavor," I said.

Her stroke drifted a little. The boat fell out of sync.

"Hold," I said, feathering my paddle flat. We coasted to a gentle standstill, the mass of kelp taking our weight as if it had been waiting for us. "You have something on your mind. Talk to me."

She looked past me toward the strait, jaw set in that way that says the words are sorting themselves. "I've been thinking about my sister," she said. "Mariah."

Scene 3 — Mariah's Letter

She unzipped the small pouch clipped under her spray skirt and pulled out a folded letter sealed in a plastic sleeve. The paper had been creased and re-creased. She passed it to me but kept a finger on the corner a beat longer than necessary. "I received this letter last week. before I left the City." Then she began to read.

Dear Mandi,

The horses are doing fine, especially the Premarin colt, **Promise**. He's growing into a confident, social creature—and I believe our **natural Sweet Grass** has something to do with it. When the blades are bruised they carry a light vanilla scent, not pungent but clear. My research group has isolated a **potential alkaloid** in the Sweet Grass—something that seems to stimulate interaction in the draft horses. After eating the grass, they seek each other out more. They're more attentive to humans. This is not true in the control group that eat hay and feed additives.

We have **two problems**. First, we can't isolate the alkaloid with certainty. My team is good, but we need someone with deeper **pharmacognosy / alkaloid botany** experience. Do you know anyone?

Second, I think someone—or something—is trying to shut down our work. I don't want to scare you, but there have been **odd signs** around the ranch—watching, petty damage, the feeling of being followed. It may be nothing, but I fear **equine corporations** could take destructive action if they think the grass changes how horses connect.

Please visit **soon. Love, always,** Mariah

Mandi folded the letter back along its tired seams. Her eyes were bright but steady. "JP, she needs your help," she said. "She doesn't exaggerate. For her to write this—it's serious."

We let the bull kelp cradle the kayak. The water made its quiet sounds against the hull, a soft tapping like a clock deciding to be generous. I thought of a colt named Promise nosing through a stand of grass that smelled like vanilla and of a sister who had never asked for more than the truth.

"Then we go," I said.

We re-seated our paddles and turned the bow toward Roche Harbor. The sun hung high as before, but the day had shifted its weight. Our strokes matched, not hurried—purposeful. Whatever waited for Mariah, we would be at her side soon.

CHAPTER 5

Shadows at Sunset

Recap: On the waters near Fidalgo Island, beauty and unease drift together on the tide.

Scene 1 — Evening Reflections

By the time we got home the bay had taken on its late light—rose-gold on the riffles, a thin sheen that made everything seem closer. I set a **Baylight Cellars Pinot Noir** into the cedar bucket with ice and brought two glasses to the deck. The air held that clean edge it gets after a bright day, and the rocking chairs waited where they always did, turned just enough toward each other that a conversation doesn't have to work hard.

Earlier—after the paddle and the letter—we flew the Caravan back to Anacortes. I taxied into the boathouse, tied her down, and shut down the panel. Neither of us was ready to sit still yet, so we traded floatplane for the **Buick Reatta convertible** and headed north along **Chuckanut Drive**.

Madrona tree trunks leaned over the water like they were listening, cinnamon bark peeling in scrolls; sandstone bluffs showed their ribs; turnouts opened to **Samish Bay** where the tide stitched foam into the cobbles. On a south-facing slope above the water we stopped at Baylight's little vineyard and tasting room. The winemaker poured from a bottle pulled from a quiet fridge and said the same thing everyone who farms this coast learns: the **marine air slows ripening**— cool nights, long light—so the **Pinot** keeps its brightness and doesn't get lazy. We bought the bottle, drove the last curves with the top down—the air full of cedar, salt, and warm rock—and then headed home.

Now the chairs took us in. Mandi sat first and pulled the blanket over her knees. When I eased into the other chair and leaned to pour, the western light caught her hair. For a breath it flared—a soft halo—and I stopped with the bottle in my hand.

"You're glowing," I said. "The sun setting in back of the house is reflecting back to us and setting you aglow."

She laughed, low. "JP, just pour the wine."

"Important cargo requires inspection." I finished the pour and handed her a glass. "All right— give me your read."

She tilted, swirled, and took a measured sip. "**Nose:** black raspberry, dried rose, a little coastal sage. **Palate:** medium-bodied, bright acid, fine tannin; red cherry and cranberry up front, blackberry in the middle. **Oak:** if there's any, it's neutral—just a frame. **Finish:** clean and long with that **salt-air minerality** you only get here."

I looked at her. "Since when do you talk like a sommelier?"

"A what?" she exclaimed.

"An old French wine taster." I replied.

"Oh! I thought you were swearing. I learned my wine tasting expertise in New York City." she said, amused. "Board dinners, donor events, a friend who ran a wine bar. I had to learn something besides spreadsheets."

We let another sip answer for the day: silk over the tongue, blackberries, a lift of coastal herbs, and that place-driven minerality the winemaker promised. Ferries stitched their careful lines across the outer water. The refinery stacks to the south clicked from day to evening, small lights pricking on like a map finding its towns. Somewhere below us the tide turned; you could hear it in the way the eddies changed their mind under the pilings.

"It was worth the drive," she said, looking at the glass and then at me.

We didn't hurry the second pour. Rockers found their pace. The bottle sweated gently in the cedar bucket and gave off the faintest scent of wood. For a while we talked about the road—the hairpins cut into sandstone, cyclists drafting in the lee of the bluffs, **oyster beds** showing dark at the margins of the bay. Then the light thinned and the day made room for the thing we needed to say next.

Scene 2 — The Real Danger

Twilight took the color out of things, and with it we let the conversation step from easy to exact.

"Reclassifying horses from livestock to social animals," Mandi said, "changes everything."

I nodded for her to keep going.

"Feed pens leading to slaughterhouses would end. 'Byproduct' additives in food and veterinary pharmaceuticals—gone. But the loophole stays unless someone closes it: horses fattened in U.S. feedlots still shipped to **Canada and Mexico** for slaughter."

"The corporations don't want that loop closed," I said.

"Exactly." She set her glass down, elbows on the arms of the chair. "They argue **horses can't communicate**—not in any way that rises above instinct. If Mariah's work shows they can, if she can demonstrate coordinated behavior and responsive attention after Sweet Grass exposure, the whole foundation cracks."

"Communication isn't philosophy," I said. "It's evidence. Interactions we can measure. If Promise seeks contact, if a herd changes spacing, if attention to humans increases in consistent ways—this is data."

"And data can change definitions," she said.

We listened to a tug working south with a barge, the slow mechanical heartbeat riding the water. Stars began to sort themselves in the east.

The last of the wine caught that faint starlight and made a thin ribbon of brightness at the rim.

"Pressure will escalate when they sense what she's doing," I said. "Whoever sent the arrows won't be the last to make a point."

"She won't stop," Mandi said. Not hopeful, not defiant—just sure. "But she needs help—lab help, legal help, and someone who knows how these battles are fought when nobody admits they're happening."

I let the chair rock once and stop. "Then we don't make her stand there alone."

Mandi looked over, the light almost gone from her eyes and something steadier taking its place. "We go to Montana," she said.

"We go," I said.

We sat with that a while, the decision taking its shape between us. No lists yet. No calls. Just the quiet agreement you feel in your chest when the right next step arrives and asks nothing more than acceptance.

Down in the boathouse a small wave found the ramp and spoke in the language of wood and water. The bottle in its bucket had gone cool and dark. I poured what remained, split even without having to think about it.

"To Mariah," she said.

"To Promise," I added.

We touched the glasses once—no flourish—and drank.

By the time the final glow left the horizon, I knew one thing for certain: **we'd be going to Montana.**

CHAPTER 6

Shadows on the Danube

Recap: Friendship, suspicion, and hidden motives surface in quiet exchanges.

Scene 1 — Departure from Vienna

June had warmed Vienna, but at 2400 hours the Danube still carried a midnight chill in its skin. The 330X Defender—a low-slung security craft—waited at the pier below Vienna's Donau Tower. Its twin engines purred at idle as Georg Messenger stepped aboard with a duffel and a suit bag.

At the helm stood **Captain Helmut Beck**—childhood friend, man of the river, and the reason this run could be made without notice. His blond beard caught the dock lights; years on the water had weathered his face without wearing it down. Leathery hands rested easy on the throttles.

Beck's outfit—**River Security**—had grown out of his family's barge fleet. In the nineties, it was piracy; these days the contracts were **anti-smuggling and counter-trafficking escorts**, quiet watches on sensitive cargo, and pulling boats out of trouble before trouble noticed. He ran mixed civilian crews, unarmed on commercial charters and licensed to carry sidearms only when posted with ministries. His boats were set up like discreet patrol craft: **baffled exhausts** for noise discipline, **forward-looking infrared** for night runs, disciplined **AIS** use per corridor rules, and tight comms that kept chatter off open channels. Helmut believed in prevention over confrontation—the kind of reputation that kept trouble two bends away.

"Two hours if we push her," Beck said, voice low.

"We'll keep it quiet," Messenger said. "The Abbey bells strike at noon. I can't be late."

Beck eased the Defender into the current. The bow rose as he brought her to **thirty knots**, then eased back to **twenty-eight knots** with a glance at the gauges. "Top is forty," he said, "but at midnight you listen for flotsam and driftwood—and for people who'd rather not hear us."

The city slid astern—bridges and cranes and the gold haze of Vienna at night. Ahead, **113 kilometers** of river lay ahead, leading to the **Altenwörth Lock**.

Scene 2 — The Lock and Hans

An hour upriver the lock walls shouldered into view. Beck throttled back and brought the Defender alongside a barge waiting in the chamber. A rope ladder slapped the Defender's rail.

By chance the skipper was Beck's younger brother, **Hans**. Beck went up two rungs at a time. Messenger stayed in the cabin shadows; **EL'SEC** rules forbade recognition in transit. He thought the rule ridiculous. He followed rules anyway.

Locks had their own security etiquette: names kept off the radio, **lights and cameras low**, and no loitering on decks where a phone could turn a midnight run into a morning rumor. Beck swapped a word with Hans but kept the profile small; even in friendly waters, visibility was currency.

Steel gates rumbled shut. Water climbed the walls in a steady bright line. Above, voices traded work words. Messenger kept his head down and his mind on nothing.

When the upper gates parted, Beck dropped back to the Defender.

"Hans sends his regards," he said, eyes twinkling, "and a reminder not to let Consortium business ruin your health."

Messenger managed a thin smile. "He sounds like Father **Kristof** already."

Scene 3 — Wachau Memories

Back in the current the Defender came alive again. On the starboard bank the **Wachau** vineyards took shape—terraces stacked against dark hills. Beck cracked a window. A faint, floral note moved through the cabin—**grape blossoms**, more perfume than odor.

"This time of year," Beck said. "The valley carries it."

Messenger breathed in. "Not odor," he murmured. "Perfume." For a moment the weight of boards and briefings lifted and spring did the talking.

Beck idled back and let the Defender drift. The river's pull tapped the hull.

It carried them to boyhood: bicycles rattling over cobbles to **Dürnstein Castle**, wooden swords cut from fruit crates tucked into their belts, riding the hill as if astride Percheron warhorses to rescue **Richard the Lionheart** from the Castle during the Crusades.

"You always beat me," Messenger said. "Eleven to ten."

Beck chuckled. "Only because the maidens of Dürnstein cheered for me."

They laughed, and for a breath the years fell away. Then Beck brought the engines up and the Defender shouldered forward.

Scene 4 — The Chairman's Burden

Messenger fell quiet, eyes on the black water taking them west. **EL'SEC**—the **Equine Livestock Consortium**—called itself a think tank. The secrecy said otherwise. Midnight runs. No names in transit. No press. Membership unspoken even among members. It weighed more than it should have.

What troubled him was the agenda. Horses had always been his private passion—in therapy and in medicine. Yet this board's insistence on holding the **"livestock"** line against any recognition of equines as **social mammals** carried implications he was only beginning to admit.

Beck glanced over. "You're quiet, Georg. Spooky business?"

Messenger let out a dry breath that tried to be a laugh. "Horses," he said. "How spooky can that be?"

The words sounded hollow even to him. The Defender ran on into the night toward **Melk**, the river steady under the hull, the Abbey somewhere ahead waiting for noon.

Scene 5 — The Quiet Proposal

While Helmut was at the helm, Georg opened a thin envelope he had not meant to touch until after the EL'SEC meeting in Melk. Inside was a two-page brief on **Danube Pharmaceutical Company — James Pharmaceutical: Preliminary Merger Considerations**. No letterhead, only a watermark from a Vienna boutique that preferred to be known by initials.

He skimmed the columns.

Rationale: James brings U.S. regulatory muscle and North American market share; **Danube Pharmaceutical Company (DPC)** brings EU manufacturing depth and a clean biologics pipeline. Combined animal-health and women's-health lines create defensible scale. Narrative synergy: "patient-centric" and "whole-organism" therapeutics under one roof.

Philosophy (capsule): DPC starts with the **person**—genetics, environment, daily load—then backs into chemistry. Care plans pair **medication + diet + movement**, with technology serving clinicians instead of slicing care into silos. The aim is fewer hand-offs, cleaner endpoints, and products that behave in real bodies, not just in models.

Why now: Mounting scrutiny at **EL'SEC** and tightening export rules create headline risk for everyone within two steps of equine supply chains. A cross-border structure could distribute exposure and calm investors. Quiet exploration recommended prior to press or parliamentary attention.

Risks: Culture clash, antitrust in two blocs, and the optics of timing. "Any perception of using a merger to mute debate on equine classification would be unacceptable," the note warned in bold.

At the bottom, a single line: **Bradshaw is open to a discreet first conversation.**

Messenger refolded the brief and slid it back into the envelope. The cabin smelled faintly of citrus cleaner and cold metal. Above, the thrum of the engines said they were making their time.

He reached up and clicked the reading light off. Not on the river, he told himself. **Melk first.**

Then, perhaps, a call.

CHAPTER 7

EL'SEC Council Melk, Austria
Next Day — Very Early Morning

Recap: Beneath ancient stone, voices clash over the future of the horse.

Scene 1 — Arrival

Helmut did a 180-degree turn and smoothly rested his boat against the Melk landing. Georg leaped ashore. Helmut threw his bag and suit bag onto the dirt path.

Helmut asked when Georg wanted to be picked up.

"Tomorrow 1800 hours."

"Got it. See you then, Tschüss, my friend." replied Helmut

"Tschüss," Georg replied.

Georg stood for a moment at the foot of the path leading up to Melk city center.

High on the hill overlooking Melk and the Danube sat the Benediktinerstift Melk (Abbey of the Benedictine Order of Melk).

Built in 1089, it sat like a sentinel overlooking the Danube and Melk. It appeared less like a monastery and more like a fortress of faith and power. The great dome of the abbey church gleamed, while the wings of the cloister stretched in deliberate symmetry, enclosing secrets within their walls.

Monks in black habits still walked the courtyards, though tourists with cameras followed not far behind.

But behind the frescoed halls and gilded altars, there were rooms unseen by the public— vaulted chambers with thick oak doors, the kind that had survived invasions, wars, and regimes. Here, the Equine Livestock Strategic Consortium gathered. The abbey, with its thousand years of history, provided both cover and legitimacy. To the casual visitor, it was a monument to God. To the initiated, it was also a place where international power brokers spoke freely, knowing the walls themselves had long practice in keeping silence.

The walk to the Abbey was a familiar walk. Childhood ventures came back to him, river smells mixing with the woods lining the River. He looked to his right and there was the Pub that Helmut and he used to play hide and seek. An old sign announced Die Donauwelle (*The Danube Wave*) with its wide terrace, low whitewashed walls, colorful umbrellas. The Danube almost lapped at the edge of the garden.

At a fast pace Georg walked the 1,000 yards to the little bridge that flowed over a Danube tributary into the city of Melk. Before he arrived at the stairs to the Abbey he passed the **Apotheke Messinger**, his father's pharmacy.

He knew he did not have the time to stop but he was drawn to the window.

Looking inside he took a moment to daydream or better yet since it was night, to night-dream.

The scent of the Apotheke was always the first thing that struck him: sharp camphor, sweet lavender, bitter valerian, alcohol, and ink. A thousand years of plant and powder distilled into air.

Tall shelves of dark wood lined the walls, each filled with brown-glass bottles and porcelain jars labeled in Latin: *Tinctura Arnicae. Pulvis Digitalis. Radix Liquiritiae.* A ladder rolled along brass rails to reach the highest rows. In the front window, street light caught colored liquids arranged in display, glowing like stained glass.

At the counter, Georg's father Harry worked with steady hands. A mortar and pestle ground into rhythm, powders mixing into fine dust before being scraped onto a marble slab. Beside him, he saw himself weighing dried willow bark on brass scales, careful to balance the measure precisely. It was after the war.

"Patience, Georg," his father said, voice calm but firm. "An apothecary does not just dispense medicine. We measure, we balance, we mix, we listen." The words carried weight. Even as war had stripped the shelves of quinine and morphine, his father found substitutes. Oak bark for fever, chamomile for nerves, willow for pain. Farmers, mothers, even soldiers filled the small shop, all leaving with packets tied in paper and a quiet reassurance.

At a young age, Georg felt the pull of something larger—the new science, the future of pharmaceuticals beyond the old wooden counters. But in that moment, under his father's watch, he also felt the order, the discipline, the reverence for healing that no factory could replace.

He could still feel the weight of his father's hand on his shoulder, grounding him in the old ways.

When Georg opened his eyes, the path to the Abbey lay before him. Deep inside, **Apotheke Messinger** still lived, lit by light on colored jars, filled with the scent of trust and care.

Scene 2 — Melk Abbey Arrival

At the Abbey's red door, **Georg Messenger** knocked once, lightly. The wood answered with a long, ceremonial creak. **Abbot Kristof** stood framed in the opening—broad-shouldered beneath a flowing black Benedictine robe, eyes keen and amused.

"You look well for someone just off the river," he said, his accent warm and unhurried.

Georg smiled. "And you look exactly the same. Monks don't age?"

"Only in the knees," Kristof replied with a soft laugh, stepping back to usher him inside.

The Abbey smelled of beeswax, incense caught in stone, and the papery sweetness of old parchment. Footsteps hushed themselves on polished floors. Kristof walked beside Georg down a vaulted corridor and pointed up to a new restoration on the frescoed ceiling—angels bright again where soot had dulled them.

"In your youth," Georg said, "you were a theologian with contraband—lectures on herbal medicine, half your citations from **Apotheke Messinger** archives."

Kristof's mouth lifted. "Your father was a good man," he said as they paused by a tall window. Morning waited at the edge of it. "He sold cures, yes—but he gave people hope first. That is harder."

Georg swallowed the knot in his throat. "The shop is different now."

Kristof nodded once. "So is the world. That's why we meet in places like this."

The corridor bent toward the **Imperial Wing**—the route Emperors and Habsburg Royals once took when the stagecoach road between Vienna and Salzburg demanded a stop here. The **Marble Hall** loomed behind a carved arch. Latin on the entablature caught the eye: *Hospites tamquam Christus suscipiantur*—"Guests should be received as Christ was"; and beneath it, *Cuilibet honor suus*—"To each the honor due."

Georg's gaze climbed limestone columns and imagined monarchs at the stair, gold braid and velvet brushing rail. He slowed without meaning to.

"Stop dreaming, Georg," Kristof called over his shoulder, already past the arch. "The Imperial Suite is closed. I have a very nice monk's room for the few hours you'll sleep under God's roof. Come on, old friend."

The guest quarters were small and exacting: a narrow bed, a wooden desk, a crucifix thoughtfully placed, and a washbasin just wide enough to turn in. Kristof left him there with a blessing and a time.

Sleep came quickly. At **0600** the bells lifted him into a golden morning over the Wachau.

Scene 2 — Melk Abbey Library, Morning of the EL'SEC Meeting

The library's high, arched windows spilled light across rows of gilded spines. Dust motes moved like slow snow in the sun.

Georg sat at a carved oak table with a vellum-bound **Plantae Medicinales Alpinae** open before him. The calfskin spine creaked when he settled it flat; copperplate plates of gentians, arnica, and yarrow looked up in winter blues and greens. A monk's tidy marginalia in brown ink crawled the margins—dosages and uses in a careful Latin hand: *pro contusione: Arnica montana; pro anxietate: Valeriana officinalis; vulnera: Achillea millefolium.* **Apotheke Messinger** had once kept all three in glass apothecary jars; as a boy he'd scooped measures with a horn spoon for his father, the shop's scale ticking toward enough.

He traced the engraving of **Gentiana lutea** with a fingertip. The caption noted that bitterness teaches the tongue to pay attention. Plants taught in their own language, he thought—resins, volatiles, timing—and people learned if they were patient. **Grape blossoms** were no alpine herb, but the idea of a scent as a message was as old as the monks.

From his blazer he took a worn leather pouch and removed his grandfather's silvered compass. The double eagle of the old empire glinted at the hinge. **Josef Messenger**, naval officer, had once told him: *"The sea has no borders, but loyalty always finds its way home."*

Georg turned the compass in his palm, felt the decisiveness of its needle, then tucked it away. Duty still pulled at him, but ships and seas were gone; he was steering a council with a hidden map.

He opened his laptop and reviewed **EL'SEC**'s remit: equine oversight, regulation, preservation of **livestock classification**. He paged through minutes. Not much new: a note on hormone supply volatility, a short memo—*China further restricts racing on the mainland.*

Neutrality paid well, and neutrality was the price of the chairmanship. He didn't agree with all of it—slaughter, **Premarin**—but he wore the role as he'd been asked to wear it.

An e-mail from **Jacques** flagged itself: **Andre Laurent** intends to raise an "urgent" matter on Montana and horse cognition.

Georg closed the laptop and checked his watch. Time to walk down to the vaulted cellar.

Scene 3 — EL'SEC Meeting

The Abbey's wine cellar breathed cool air and stone. Lanterns lifted the vaults in warm ovals. Eight members of the **Equine Livestock Strategic Consortium** sat along a long oak table, their postures as revealing as their agendas.

Jacques Moreau of France dabbed at his lips with a monogrammed napkin; cured meat clung faintly to the wool of his tailored coat. In dining rooms he was eloquence and grace; in chambers like this his calculus ran cold.

Beside him, **Sir Simon Danridge**, the British Olympic dressage representative, adjusted a Union Jack lapel pin and brushed a stray horsehair from his cuff. Discipline impressed Georg; Danridge's certainty—that horses were livestock, always—did not.

Andre Laurent of Canada leaned back, arms crossed, gaze steady. Owner of one of North America's largest equine slaughter facilities, he was sparing with volume and generous with precision—the sort of man who cut through arguments without leaving fingerprints.

Dr. Tony Giovanni, American pharmacologist and **Premarin** executive, wore a practiced, persuasive smile. "Legacy drug, irreplaceable value," he liked to say. Georg had seen the foals.

Sally Glasco, from the U.S. restaurant sector, reclined and scanned as if pricing cuts: charm on television, market tactician here, a quiet advocate for legalizing horse meat in high-end dining.

Dr. Manny Lopez of Brazil scrolled a tablet, eyes narrowing. Veterinary scientist. Epidemiologist. One of the few to file a minority report opposing hormone-derived slaughter incentives. Georg admired the man's quiet courage.

Mr. Dwayne Jardine, Executive Director of Racing at the **Hong Kong Jockey Club**, sat careful and composed. Quiet could mean fear; quiet could mean strategy. With Jardine, Georg read both—and the shadow Beijing cast behind him.

At the far end, **Mr. Fathi** of the UAE—thoroughbred elite, desert-bred legacy stables—rested in the stillness of the falcon before the strike.

Georg took the chair at the head. "Thank you for coming," he said. "Let's begin."

He called first on **Jardine** for an update on China—a subject that he had noted in recent meeting minutes..

Jardine cleared his throat. Years abroad had softened his Mandarin-accented English. "In **Hong Kong**, racing continues," he said. "The Jockey Club remains the world's most profitable. Every week the stands at **Happy Valley** overflow. The wagers are legal there, unlike on the mainland. Beijing looks the other way—for now—as long as revenue stays in Hong Kong."

He paused, then went on. "Chairman, you know as well as I do that racing in China is politics. The Party banned it in **1949**—gambling made it unacceptable. The **Shanghai Racecourse**, once the pride of Asia, was erased. Where horses thundered, **People's Square** now stands. I grew up walking those same grounds with my father. He told me the

Race Club clock tower once marked the sky, but the course vanished—a warning that even proud traditions can be erased overnight."

He folded his hands. "In Hong Kong, under the Jockey Club, we kept the flame. **Happy Valley. Sha Tin.** Racing there is not only gambling—it's culture, discipline, bloodlines. Our directors carry the title **Steward**. We are custodians of a trust. And we will defend it."

The room held still. Even Danridge inclined his head.

Georg felt a flicker of memory: liberty in Hong Kong, shore leave after months at sea, a hundred thousand voices in unison at Happy Valley. He let it go. "Thank you, Mr. Jardine. Noted."

At Georg's glance, **Andre** spoke next. "Chairman, this is urgent. We must address the **Sweet Grass** operation in **Montana**."

Jacques exhaled through his nose. "We've discussed this already."

"No," Andre said, the word cut thin. "We have not discussed **new evidence**. The horse food additive corporations claim they read an article in a Purdue University Research Journal that a ranch in Big Timber has a formula where horses communicate through enhanced cognition.

The owner, **Mariah Haynes,** says she has isolated a compound and they will spur citizens to lobby for reclassification."

Sally raised an eyebrow. "Reclassified? Like whales?"

Danridge scoffed, almost on cue. "Nonsense. Horses are livestock. Period."

Dr. Lopez set his tablet down and leaned forward, tapping the table once, lightly. "Not nonsense, Sir Simon. You've heard of **CETI**—the *Cetacean Translation Initiative*. They analyze sperm-whale **codas**—clicks like Morse code. Different clans, different dialects; turn-taking, rules, signatures. Some scientists now argue it approaches a **language**." He let the word stand.

"Whales were once meat and oil," Lopez continued. "When we realized they were talking— structured, cultural communication—laws shifted. Hunting bans followed.

That precedent is precisely why Montana worries you. If **Sweet Grass** demonstrably stimulates equine cognition and structured interaction, the next question becomes: are horses livestock… or social communicators?"

Silence collected in the arches. Even Jacques stopped with the napkin.

Andre leaned in. "If labeled **social mammals**, slaughter becomes illegal. **Premarin** mares go. Restaurants lose food supply. If successful, it ends horse slaughter—mine, and perhaps yours, Jacques."

Sally lifted her glass, voice even. "On the consumption side, the American palate recoils at the word *horse* even as import numbers whisper otherwise. Close domestic slaughter and demand doesn't vanish—it crosses borders and goes underground. If classification shifts, my sector becomes radioactive for a decade. You can win a vote and still lose the culture."

Georg watched Jacques shift in his chair.

"Andre," Georg said, "urgent implies imminent threat. Evidence?"

Andre's gaze stayed steady. "Credible reports of genetic studies and behavioral trials—draft horses responding to **Sweet Grass** stimuli. Communication patterns analyzed—possibly decoded. If this catches press or political traction—"

"Thank you," Georg cut in. "Facts over hypotheticals."

Jacques leaned forward. "Mr. Chairman, I've spoken to Andre. He overstates. The science is vague. Sources unverified."

Andre's reply was flint. "Your loyalty to **foie gras** blinds you."

Georg raised a hand. "Enough. This forum demands respect." Andre subsided, but the line held between them.

"Do you have verified data?" Georg asked.

"Not yet," Andre said. "But we need **surveillance. Containment.**"

"We are not an enforcement agency," Georg said evenly. "Surveillance must be legal. If this reaches the press—"

"It won't," **Moreau** said smoothly. "We'll inquire quietly. If it's nonsense, fine. If not—be prepared."

Georg made a note. "Preliminary inquiry. Non-invasive. No threats. Agreed?" Seven nodded.
Jardine remained still.

Dr. Lopez cleared his throat. "Chair, one veterinary item for the record: **New World screwworm** pressure is rising in parts of South America and the Caribbean. It's obligate myiasis—the fly lays eggs in **fresh wounds**; the larvae consume living tissue. Cattle get the headlines, but **equines are also susceptible**. Long-haul transport and holding pens create exactly the wounds it needs. A single gravid female can seed an outbreak."

He glanced around the table. "I recommend the **Veterinary Subcommittee** step up surveillance—border alerts, mandatory wound checks on transported stock, and contingency planning with national veterinary authorities should an incursion occur."

Georg nodded. "Noted. Refer to Veterinary for surveillance and guidance."

"Then we reconvene with facts, not speculation," Georg said, and closed the agenda.

Scene 4 — Late Lunch in Melk

By late afternoon the minutes were encrypted and uploaded to the Swiss repository. Georg stepped into the sunlit plaza and found a table under the lindens. He ordered **Wiener Schnitzel** and a tall beer.

The square breathed like a single body: children tapped fingers in the fountain's cold spray; tourists drifted between shops and cafés; waiters triangulated with plates and wineglasses.

High above, the **Abbey** lifted its golden façade and chimed the late hour like a guardian carved from light.

Memory surfaced—he and **Helmut** as boys racing bicycles around this very square, two laps, then a sprint down to the Danube; on the return they'd stop by **Apotheke Messinger** for ice cream.

A loud scrape broke the afternoon. Across the plaza **Jacques** and **Andre** sat at a café table.

Andre had shoved his chair back; the wooden legs had raked the cobbles. Conversation thinned around them to a hush.

"You'll regret ignoring this," Andre said, voice controlled but hard. "Sweet Grass will be the end of all of us if we do nothing."

Jacques motioned, palm down. Sit. Breathe.

Andre felt the square's eyes and stood awkwardly over the table—a heavyset man glaring down at a perfectly groomed gentleman.

Tension radiated like static. Andre's jowls trembled; he forced a smile, lifted his hands in reassurance, and righted the chair. He sat, color high with embarrassment.

The plaza exhaled. Glassware found its rhythm again; knives met porcelain; laughter returned by degrees. The Abbey bells finished their toll.

Jacques leaned in. "André, what is wrong with you? You are not the friend—the French brother—I've always known. This Montana business is consuming your sanity."

Andre bent forward, elbows to wood, head in his hands. "I know, Jacques. But this is my survival. EL'SEC—especially you—don't understand the magnitude of what's coming."

"I am sorry, André," Jacques said softly, "but I think I do. The issue is not urgent. We have no evidence. No proof. We cannot leap blindly toward an unknown solution."

Andre's breath slowed. At last: "**Jacques, je m'excuse, mon ami.** I must catch the train to Vienna, then my flight to Quebec. My business awaits."

Andre never called it a slaughterhouse. **Packing plant** sounded cleaner, even as it disguised the truth.

He pushed back from the table with effort and gave a small bow.

Andre: "Bon, il faut que j'y aille." *(Well, I have to go.)*
Jacques: "D'accord, à plus tard." *(All right, see you later.)*
Andre: "Salut, mon ami. À bientôt." *(Bye, my friend. See you soon.)*
Jacques: "Ciao, André. Prends soin de toi." *(Bye, André. Take care of yourself.)*

Andre turned toward the **Hauptbahnhof** and began the walk to the station.

Jacques stayed behind, shaking his head.

Unseen by either Frenchman, Georg had watched the exchange. He sipped his beer and let his eyes find the ribbon of the Danube shining beyond the roofs.

Sweet Grass was not going away. Nor, he suspected, was the storm it carried.

CHAPTER 8

South of Big Timber, Montana
Early Morning

Recap: Decisions made in secret chambers begin to shape events far from view

The June sun lifted over the **Crazy Mountains**, laying a pale gold across the benches northeast of Yellowstone.

Mariah Haynes eased her **Dodge Ram** onto **Montana Route 298**, the bed crowded with brown paper sacks from Big Timber—flour, coffee, dog kibble, a case of mason jars, and a stack of fresh dish towels she'd found on sale. She was stocking up for her sister **Mandi's** visit— and for Mandi's partner, **Jean Paul**, whom she had yet to meet.

The drive south was a run she could do with her eyes closed. She passed the **Road Kill Bar & Grill** with its hand-painted sign, the tiny **Milford** post office with its single window and habit of losing track of anything that wanted tracking, and the turnoff toward **Natural Bridge State Park**, where spring melt could turn the river white and loud as faith. She preferred Milford's post office. No grid, no digital breadcrumb. Some things should stay between sender and receiver, unobserved.

Big Timber suited her—fewer than two thousand souls, ranchers and professionals braided by the same wind. In the grocery aisles she

45

waved to faces she knew; on auction days you could name nearly every ranch along the **Boulder River** by the cut of the hat and the set of the shoulders. It was the right place for **Seneca Ranch**—sanctuary, research, and a home that slept guests when she ran out of daylight. Far enough from **Livingston's** summer gridlock to hear herself think.

She smiled, remembering how she'd chosen this valley: irrigation from the river, room to rotate pastures, neighbors who could fix a carburetor and a fence in the same morning, and universities willing to send hands eager to learn.

Purdue's veterinary program had backed her grant work; **Montana State** lay an hour up the road with grad students who thought nothing of calving-season hours and field notebooks smudged with mud.

The highway curled. Wide hay meadows took the light and shivered under it. A **kestrel** hung like a pendant over a fencepost, wings beating, then dropped into the grass. **Alfalfa** rode the breeze through her open window, mixed with the dry pepper of dust when she turned onto **Knight of Dreams Road**. Gravel clicked the fenders. Ahead, the timber arch came into view—two uprights carved by local hands, flanking a beam where four wooden draft horses kept watch: **Percheron, Belgian, Shire, Clydesdale**. They looked like a benediction in place. Beyond the arch the spring pastures spread green and yellow against the far snow. The first heads lifted as the Ram rolled by.

Promise was the first to break into trot—sleek young Percheron, black coat taking the sun like oil. His dam, **Molly Belle**, grazed near him, still keeping a mother's perimeter.

The memory of Molly Belle's trip to Seneca Ranch came full as the road bent: a **bitter winter day** at the Montana feedlot, pens crowded with underfed drafts, heads tipped against a wind that came with teeth.

Mariah had walked the line naming the things she could fix and the things she could not. One mare lifted her gaze and met her square. Percheron, she thought. **Premarin** mare—she knew the back tattoo, the roster number: **#1,479**.

She had stepped to the barbed wire and the mare had come as far as bruised skin would let her, muzzle over the wire, forehead exposed like a question nobody wanted to ask.

Mariah set her palm on the horses forehead, the broad center where memory and spirit meet.

For a moment the cold went somewhere else. The ears softened, the eyes half-closed.

Something passed between them—older than language, older than auctions and lot numbers.

She leaned her own forehead to the mare's and knew it before she knew how she knew it. She pulled back, startled at herself, and said it in a whisper as if saying it too loud would make it untrue. "You're **pregnant**."

The mare's eyes softened further, a small acknowledgment, and the wind paused long enough for Mariah to feel what she was obligating herself to do.

Pregnant mares weren't supposed to be there. If the rancher had known, they'd have held her to foal and sold the pair by the pound.

The auction dragged. When **#1,479** finally came up, Mariah felt the room tilt. The bidding found its pitch, and when the gavel fell she knew the mare belonged to her.

Outside, before the trailer, she pressed her forehead to the mare's again. "I can't keep calling you **#1,479**," she said. The mare leaned in as if to push a syllable into Mariah's chest. The name floated up from whatever place names live before they are spoken. **Molly Belle.**

"You're safe now, Molly Belle," Mariah said. "You'll foal under open pasture, with the mountains looking on."

The tension unhooked from the mare's shoulders. She walked the ramp and did not look back.

That was how **Promise** began—under snow sky, a dark colt with a mouth that learned quickly where the milk lived, a temperament even then that wanted company.

Mariah let the Ram idle at the rise where the ranch opened in full. Ahead of her the **Boulder River** finished a long riffle under willows and aspens, throwing silver at the sun. The sound of it carried up the slope. The ranch log house took the knoll as if it had always been there—**broad deck** reaching toward the water like the bow of a slow boat. On summer evenings the deck caught gold until the last of it slid west behind the ridge.

Knight of Dreams stood beyond on his own acre, white as a page with the first snow on it, watching in the way of elders who know a thing about mornings.

Rescued decades earlier in Santa Barbara, he had outlived neglect and more than one winter to become a kind of gravity on the place. Past his thirtieth year, his pasture was his own—though somehow, most mornings, the gate stood open and the herd gathered around him, as if to take attendance.

She rolled forward. The road narrowed to shadow as it sidled the river. The sound of water thickened, mingling with the crunch of gravel.

The **log house** came between cottonwoods, and beyond it, tucked to the slope, the low-slung **research lab** wore its earth-tones like camouflage. Between house and lab the pastures rolled away—fifty acres of **Sweet Grass** set like a quilt.

Here, even with windows closed, the place had a **scent** all its own. Not pungent—never loud— but identifiable the way a song is. A small, clean note of **vanilla and clover** that seemed to live wherever the Sweet Grass lived. When the wind was right, you could find a field by it with your eyes shut. When it was wrong, it still found you.

She parked by the garage and killed the engine. Two rescue dogs—**Maria** and **Max**— materialized from under the porch and did the inventory: new smells on her boots, the honest evidence of other dogs somewhere between town and here, and a fleeting interest in the bag that held treats.

"Greeters," she said. Their tails answered yes.

Inside, the great room smelled of pine logs and last night's fire gone to ash. The **mantel** carried frames—rescued horses with their winter coats still shaggy, students in borrowed slickers smiling around a stuck pickup, **Knight** standing thin but tall in a storm. The **rocking chairs** had their stack of journals beside them, spines broken to favorite pages.

She set the sacks on the counter, put perishables in the fridge, and stood at the big window a moment. From there the view fell to the pastures, the river flashing, and the **deck** throwing its long line over the bank. On quiet evenings she stood on that deck and let the river's song go through her; the horses grazed in the near field, and the **Crazy Mountains** took the stars without apology.

Now **Promise** stood in the center of the herd with **Knight** near, the others arranged with the purpose that looks like casualness until you learn to read it. Heads went up, ears moved, weight shifted.

It was almost **lunchtime for Maria and Max**, and some communications required no laboratory.

"Almost there, boys," she said, and heard herself laugh. "I won't forget you."

Seneca Ranch had grown into more than a place to keep horses safe. The log home had been built to **welcome**—students, visiting researchers, a lost tourist when the weather turned, and sometimes the heaviest guests of all: those who were arriving at the end of their road.

One wing held a **hospice suite** arranged with the same care she gave her horses. **Sunlight** came clean through tall windows that looked to the pastures. A quilt pieced by ranch women lay folded at the foot of the bed. Photographs on the walls showed horses and open fields— pictures chosen to let someone travel far without moving. A narrow door opened to a **private deck** just wide enough for a wheelchair; from there the **Boulder** River spoke loud enough to be a comfort.

There was almost always someone in that room. On good days the staff wheeled a patient out into the pasture. The horses came slow and deliberate, lowering their heads into a lap to be stroked. Others would **nicker** and hold, as if they understood there was an order to things and today it was not about them. In those moments Mariah felt communication in a way that left no room for doubt. Science would catch up. It would have to.

Across the river, the lab tucked into the hillside with a deck over the spring current. From that deck you could see how the **Sweet Grass** moved in a wind—the way the blades leaned together and then apart like breath.

Students charted it, counted intervals, coded behavior. Some days the data were numbers and graphs. Some days they were written in the way a horse walked across a field to stand beside another horse who didn't know it needed company until it had it.

She carried the last sacks into the pantry and checked the list on the chalkboard: oats, farrier tomorrow, **Purdue** call at noon, change filters in the water system, check the **collars** on the three mares in the test rotation. On the far edge of the board, someone had drawn a heart and inside it written **MB + P**. Molly Belle and Promise.

Back at the window, the herd had shifted again. Promise tossed his head, a show-off flick he'd had since he was small. Beyond them a small gust passed over the **Sweet Grass**, and for a second the air in the kitchen picked up that mild **vanilla-clover** note, the one that was always there where the grass was. It felt like a sign, though she told herself she didn't need signs.

The dogs had already guessed the next task and trotted ahead. At the feed room she measured grain, listening to the river the way people listen to weather and prayer.

Out in the sun she called the first names and the herd answered in motion—lines that looked like joy drawn across a field.

Her work had taken years—grants that died at a committee table, nights so quiet she could hear her own ribs count, trade-offs she tried not to keep score on. She had chosen this.

Sometimes she wondered if she had traded **motherhood** for it. Then Promise threw his head again and came in at a trot that had room for her in it, and she knew she had made her choice long ago and kept making it.

Seneca Ranch was redemption—for the horses, certainly; for her, possibly; and for anyone who still believed in second chances. The river said the same thing in its own language as it went on by.

CHAPTER 9

Slaughterhouse Canada
Same Day – Afternoon

Recap: Research deepens, but so too does the shadow of those who would silence it.

Scene 1 — *J'aime Les Chevaux*

Andre Laurent arrived at his Canadian-licensed *J'aime Les Chevaux* (translated, "I Love Horses") slaughterhouse outside Quebec City.

He looked every bit the European industrialist—slicked-back silver hair, tailored wool scarf, Italian shoes untouched by the grime of the pens.

Pulling on a floor-length coverall, he stepped just beyond the antiseptic glare of the processing floor. Stainless steel and blood-washed concrete stretched beneath the hum of machinery.

Steam rose from drains, carrying the sour tang of ammonia and blood.

From the catwalk, he paused to watch the line. A Percheron mare, ribs faintly showing under her gray coat, balked at the chute. Two men with paddles slapped her hindquarters until she lurched forward. Her ears shot back, eyes rolling white, nostrils flaring with panic. She reared once, hooves striking sparks on steel, before the pneumatic gate slammed shut behind her. The dull thud of the captive bolt echoed, followed by silence broken only by the whine of chains.

Andre didn't flinch. Compassion was for people who couldn't afford control.

He turned away, tossing the coverall aside as he crossed to the administration building. Staff rose automatically at his approach; he dismissed them with a flick of his hand.

His corner office was a monument to dominance: a red cedar desk upholstered in Percheron hide. His secretary, Cheri, tried to greet him, but he ignored her, closing the door behind.

He knew what he had to do. The Sweet Grass project in Montana was a threat. In his circles, he'd heard of a firm—shadowy, dangerous—that "solved" such problems.

He tapped his phone. "Wainwright & Winchester?" "Yes."

"This is Monsieur Andre Laurent. I need to speak with Mr. Wainwright or Mr. Winchester." "There is no one by those names."

"Wait. I need to place a contract. An emergency."

A pause. Then a flat reply: "Yes. What do you want?"

Wainwright & Winchester—known only as W&W—were legends in whispers. They specialized in weaponized misinformation: distorting truth, destroying reputations, erasing opponents without leaving fingerprints.

"A woman named Mariah Haynes," Andre said quickly. "Draft horse sanctuary in Montana. Researching horse cognition. If successful, horses could be reclassified—no longer livestock. We want her silenced. Final result: she renounces her findings and stops her program."

The reply from W&W, "Price is one million euros plus expenses. Up front. No discussion. Send proposal."

"Agreed," replied Andre expecting more of a conversation.

Click.

Andre's hands trembled. He had neither EL'SEC's approval nor the funds. W&W didn't answer when he called back. He was bound.

He wrote the request, sent it, and immediately sought financing. A trusted banker—an old ally—approved a €2M loan using *J'aime Les Chevaux* as collateral.

At home, his wife Shirley barely looked up from *Star Trek: Through the Wormhole*. She cared only that the money flowed in her direction.

Andre caught his reflection in the bathroom mirror: bloated, pale, exhausted. He sank into his Jacuzzi, then the sauna, trying to sweat out panic.

He whispered to the cedar walls: *This is not murder. This is business. She's a threat to everything we've built. Better her dream dies than my empire.*

But the words dissolved in the steam. The panic clung to him like a second skin. He went to bed without looking at the mirror again.

Scene 2 — Destroyers

In a remote, luxurious cabin south of Great Falls, Montana—off State Route 89—a hidden dirt road branched subtly from the highway. Almost invisible when driving south, it appeared to be a simple continuation of the main road. In the winter and heading north snow blanketed both paths, making it easy to miss the turn off.

A mile down this offshoot stood a weathered wooden gate, designed to appear like a cattle barrier but in truth was meant to discourage intruders. The gate was reinforced steel camouflaged as wood, with hair-thin copper wires laced through its crossbeams, connected to a generator deep in the woods. If activated, it could deliver a non-lethal but incapacitating shock. Fortunately, no unwanted visitors had ever tested it.

Beyond the gate, the road twisted through thick forest for ten miles, eventually opening into a clearing with three buildings: a large log cabin, a barn, and a supply shed. Behind them loomed the foothills of the Little Belt Mountains.

From the outside, the structures looked abandoned—weather-beaten, fenced with rusted barbed wire, and posted with aging *No Trespassing* signs.

Inside, however, the cabin was a marvel of clandestine technology and comfort. Custom- designed to appear dilapidated from the outside, its windows were reflective glass to mask the interior while giving occupants full visibility of the outside.

Within, it was a high-tech fortress.

At a tall table in the "war room"—a space anchored by a repurposed acrylic-coated ship hatch—sat Pete and Jake.

The surrounding walls were lined with high-resolution monitors displaying live feeds, encrypted messages, and news broadcasts of previous projects. At the moment, one screen replayed a recent news broadcast about a sabotage incident that Jake had pulled off.

"That was a good job, Jake," Pete said, a rare note of praise in his voice. "You're getting better with pyrotechnics. Pulled us a clean 35 grand."

Jake, whose mental elevator didn't quite reach the top floor but who excelled in explosives, beamed. "Thank you, Pete."

Pete Jones and Jake Smith were aliases. Pete was really Peter Alexander of Nantucket Island; Jake, Jeremiah Mansfield from Coeur d'Alene, Idaho.

Six months a year, they were contractors for hire—saboteurs, enforcers, covert operatives. The other half, they returned to their separate lives. Pete maintained a cover story about energy exploration to pacify his disinterested wife; Jake lived as a hermit.

They operated by handler contracts—anonymous digital messages via an untraceable satellite channel. Their satellite dish, hidden high in a pine tree, relayed these messages through a secure link to a decoder in the cabin.

The cabin, although rough on the outside, was equipped with advanced amenities. Each had a personal suite with a home theater, workout room, and a 360° immersive jogging simulator.

Jake's simulator featured a custom-designed fantasy route built from red-light districts across the globe. The AI software rendered lifelike encounters, allowing Jake to indulge his imagination.

Pete, on the other hand, used his jogging room to run the built-in landscapes and preferred classical music during cardio.

When they had a contract the video was uploaded and they could actually use the 360 degree immersive simulator to practice the destruction.

The kitchen was split—each man had his own fridge, microwave, and automated meal prep buttons. With cases of frozen meals and beer, they were self-sufficient. They took no chances with illness, having learned the hard way when Pete once broke his leg chopping firewood.

The handlers' response to a problem was chilling: *Fix it yourselves. Seek no outside help. Secure link will be terminated if breached.*

Together, they were efficient and brutal, compartmentalizing their work from their personal animosities. During missions, they had each other's backs. Between jobs, they coexisted.

Off the kitchen was their costume storage, housing various disguises. Once used, these were either burned or discarded to eliminate any trace.

The great room was their shared planning space. It was the only area where collaboration occurred. Here, they researched targets and coordinated logistics for missions—always under the handlers' cryptic direction.

Currently, each was immersed in a personal movie—Pete watching *Star Trek 20: Rebirth of Vulcan*, Jake watching *Hangover 20: Ten Days of Amnesia.* Their 4D helmets engaged (sight, sound, scent, and sensation).

Suddenly, sirens blared, red lights spun, and the Blackhawks goal horn filled the cabin. The alert meant one thing: a new contract had arrived.

Jake and Pete simultaneously tore off their helmets, startled yet conditioned. The cabin had awakened. A new mission had begun.

Scene 4 — Contract Confirmed

They rushed to the great room where the only phone was located. One of their agreements was to have only one landline phone and the only mode was hands-free speakerphone. They did not trust each other to answer it alone.

They sat at the Contract Strategic Planning table. The red light on the phone station flashed. Pete pushed the button.

"Pete and Jake here," he said.

"W&W," replied the distorted voice of Sam.

"Yes."

"Are you free to accept a contract?"

"Affirmative."

"One question. Are you located near Big Timber, Montana?"

A typical. Normally there were no questions. After *Affirmative*, the call would drop, and a contract would follow.

Pete and Jake looked at each other.

"Well?" Sam pushed.

Jake nodded.

"Yes," Pete replied.

Hal said, "One other piece of information"

Pete and Jake looked at each other their facial expressions expressed their feelings of okay here it comes, the kicker."

"Go ahead." Replied Pete.

"We have read some research reports that the research is on horse reclassification by the government. This has gotten the feed Additive corporations upset.

They have contracted an ex-salesman to scare the owner. We have learned through our intelligence network that this ex- salesman is firing arrows with scary notes tied to the shaft into the owners pasture."

"Say what!" said Jake.

"I know." said Hal. "It sounds crazy but there it is. I don't think it will interfere with your plans. Just go ahead and follow the contract. Don't get bogged down with the corporations Halloween tricks."

Hal paused, "Okay?"

Pete said, "Okay."

"Fine. Contract incoming." The call ended.

Jake grumbled, "You don't even know where Big Timber is."

Pete was already pulling up maps. "Not far. Just east on I-90. Maybe fifty miles."

Jake perked up. "No flights? Great!"

"Yeah, great—and bad," Pete muttered. "It's too close to the cabin. Too easy to bring heat back here."

Jake shrugged. "Let's at least read it."

An alert flashed: ENCRYPTED CONTRACT DOWNLOADING.

Pete entered the password. The contract read:

Destroy a researcher's reputation to end her equine behavioral studies. Objective: she abandons all research. Target: Mariah Haynes, Seneca Ranch. GPS coordinates provided. Lethal force not permitted for target, but collateral damage acceptable. Payment: $50K in advance. Costs covered by fee. Signify acceptance.

"Not much to go on," Jake said.

Pete said nothing, thinking it over. It looked straightforward. Minimal travel. Possibly Jake could handle it solo.

"Jake, I think it's a go. Do you agree?"

Jake didn't really care. "Yep." He slipped back to his movie.

Pete shook his head. "Idiot," he muttered, then typed their response:

Accepted.

Pete leaned back, folding his arms. "Same drill as always. We work it in steps."

Jake nodded, already half-distracted by his movie helmet.

Pete said, "Jake pay attention. We do what we always do, plan the stages we need to do to fulfill the contract/ I suggest three Plans."

"Jake, are you paying attention?. "Yes I hear you."

"How about: since we know about the Corporate pasture arrow with notes firing. We call that Plan A. What ever happens with Plan A happens. We are not involved.

"Plan B,"

Jake cut in, grinning. "Light something up."

Pete's mouth tightened but he didn't argue. "Right. Force them to stop the work. If that still doesn't end it—"

"Plan C," Jake finished, eyes bright. "The fun one."

"Yes," said Pete, "We take out the Ranch."

"Exactly. But remember—our handlers said the target stays alive. Collateral's fair game. Don't forget that."

Jake shrugged. "Yeah, yeah."

The words hung in the air, as the cabin's red light slowly dimmed back to calm.

CHAPTER 10

Plan B: Through the Sage
Three Days Later — Early Morning

Recap: Threads of science and sabotage tighten toward collision.

Scene 1 — The Approach

"Goddamn country," **Jake Mansfield** muttered, levering himself out of the driver's seat into cold air. "Who the hell chooses to live here? Masochists."

The **GPS** pulsed a cold blue dot on the dash: **0.10 mi** to the launch point. From there, four hundred yards to the small white barn in **Knight of Dreams'** pasture he'd marked from a satellite printout. Five hundred total.

Just inside his comfort radius with the **FOB** shaft he'd tuned—flat trajectory, heavy front. Not about precision. About **impact**.

He killed the engine and let the truck tick itself quiet.

Sagebrush ran in seams between basalt and cheatgrass. He pulled the duffel, the bow case, and started across the low ground.

Jake was built like a guard trapped in a lineman's body—six-foot-two, **250** pounds when he was behaving.

Two knee blowouts had torn the scholarship out of him before college had time to start. The pills that got him through the second season had stayed, making a home in the drawer by the bed and then in his pocket, parceled now by a partner who counted everything.

Pete had a way of noticing what a man couldn't do and finding work that made it not matter.

Jake took the steps that carried the risk. Pete took what came off the top. The arrangement made sense because Pete said it did and because Jake didn't like the feeling of being the one who had to think two moves ahead.

He stumbled in the half-light and went down hard on a knuckled shelf of **basalt**. A tear opened his jeans and bit his shin. He hissed, probed the cut with two fingers, and decided the pain **pills** had earned their keep.

He had read an article that old cowboys used sage as aftershave. He paused and cupped a sprig of **sage** in his palm. He crushed it slowly until the resin wet his fingers, then brought it to his jaw and rubbed it along the stubble.

The sting was small but clear. The smell—sharp, bitter, clean—settled him in a way he couldn't explain. He did it again, slower, and the nerves in his shoulders eased. He filed it under *things that work, though I don't know why* and slipped two sprigs into his pocket.

The GPS chirped again—**twenty feet**, then the mark. Too loud. He thumbed it silent and crouched.

Scene 2 — The Shot

He set the duffel behind a juniper and unzipped the bow case. The **arrow** had its own cradle— a custom FOB shaft, fletching kept minimal, nose weighted by the **surprise** that made this Plan B.

A thumbnail GPS chip sat under a strip of tape on the mid-shaft. He'd launched the same setup at the gravel pit a dozen times. Big target. Broadside hits. The math checked out.

He sighted on the pale rectangle of the barn's white boards through a low break in the brush.

The early light was dim. The wind was light.

Three seconds. No mistakes.

He struck the **fuse** and watched it take, a thin bead of orange eating along a black thread.

He **nocked**. **Drew**. The bow stacked weight against his shoulders in a way that made the rest of the world fall away. When the sight ring steadied on the rectangle of wall, he let his fingers widen.

Release.

The arrow left clean, fuse trailing.

Jake was moving before the sound ever came—duffel up, bow cased by touch, boots taking the slope he'd picked on the way in. Thorns scratched his forearms. Behind him the air opened with a deep crack. Heat hit the back of his neck.

He didn't turn. He didn't need to. A second later a **fireball** took the cold edge off the morning, and the plume rose and darkened.

Scene 3 — The Runout

He cut a diagonal for the wash that led back toward the road and took the worst of the **sage** across his sleeves. Smoke moved fast in this country, and he could taste the difference between plant and paint without ever having to learn the vocabulary for it. The oil-metal edge said he hadn't just started a brush problem. He'd hit **barn**.

From beyond the ridge a chorus of **dogs** cut loose—first one, then three, then however many lived along this valley answering one another, the sound stacking into a single alarm. In the pastures to his left, the horses startled and turned; hooves thudded.

He slid the last yard down to the truck on his backside, gravel and cheatgrass trying to make a home in his palms.

The **key fob** chirped, he winced at the noise, and then the engine turned and gave him the familiar rough idle he trusted when nothing else felt trustworthy.

He drove out slow to start—no rooster tails, no heroics—then put the bend in the road between the plume and his rearview. Only when asphalt replaced gravel did he let the needle rise.

His phone buzzed once in his pocket.

Pete: *Status?*

Jake kept his eyes on the road and tapped the two words he knew were expected. *All good.*

He turned onto the logging road toward the cabin. Pete would be waiting. He rolled the window down and let the **acrid** mix of burned sage and chemical smoke out of the cab.

Scene 4 — The Wake-Up

Back at **Seneca Ranch**, the blast arrived a half-second after the light—**pressure** moving faster than sound.

In the house the dogs were already up and at the door, nails *tick-tick-tick* on the floorboards.

At the pasture fence, **Promise** flung his head and planted all four feet, looking for the thing a horse can't see but can't ignore.

Farther back, the elder white head of **Knight of Dreams** lifted and held, the herd gathered near him.

The **Boulder River** kept its voice, but the valley now had a second one—the thin broken wail of **sirens** far to the south, carried long on morning air.

On the ridge a column of smoke climbed. Over the north pasture a spray of bright **splinters** had lifted and fallen—**Knight's barn**. For a breath-long beat everyone on the place thought the old horse was inside.

In the truck, with the ridge in his mirror, Jake turned north toward the cabin, where Pete was waiting.

CHAPTER 11

Seneca Ranch, Big Timber, MT

Recap: At dawn, fire shatters the calm and forces the ranch into desperate action.

Scene 1 — Morning: Explosion

Mariah jolted upright as the blast shook her cabin.

"What the hell—?"

She ran to the window. Flames clawed the sky from the direction of Knight's barn. Smoke twisted into the dawn light over the Crazy Mountains.

Across the ranch, chaos broke out as bunkhouse staff scrambled—some tossed from bed, others tangled in blankets. The alarm clanged.

The volunteer fire brigade was at least thirty minutes out. Containment would be up to them.

Training took over. Pumps kicked in, hoses uncoiled, staff in boots and pajamas braced against heat and smoke.

Son, the ranch director, swung the Quick Response truck into position and hit the pump. A torrent of water roared.

The air burned their lungs; resinous smoke mixed with the acrid bite of charred hay. Sparks snapped like gunfire as the barn's roof sagged and collapsed inward. Tar bubbled along the shingles, running in black rivulet's down the walls. Each gust of wind sent glowing cinders spiraling across the pasture, forcing staff to slap them out with coats and shovels. Horses screamed in chorus, high and panicked, the sound piercing even above the roar of fire and pump.

By the time the Big Timber firetruck finally drew near, the blaze was mostly controlled—only a skeleton of beams hissing under the spray. Silence fell, broken only by neighs—sharp, frightened, alive.

Someone shouted, "Has the Yellowstone caldera erupted?" Panic surged—then recognition. If that had happened, they would all be cinders, as would most of the United States.

Voices rose as one: "It is Knight's barn! Where is Knight? We can't find Knight." Everyone assumed Knight had been in the barn and perished.

Mariah spun in panic, pleading.… "No, not Knight of Dreams. Please, God."

Her knees buckled, and she pressed a soot-streaked hand to her chest, feeling her heartbeat hammering against her ribs. For an instant the world blurred—barn, mountains, sky—until all that remained was the void where Knight should have been.

Memories rushed in: his muzzle nudging her shoulder, his steady presence on long nights, the bond that had steadied her through grief. Losing him would mean losing the heart of the ranch itself.

The smoke blanketed the pasture, turning Seneca Ranch into a fog.

The wind gradually carried it away, whipping in circles. At the far end of the pasture, a pale figure emerged.

One of the staff on the hill strained to see, then shouted: "It's Knight! Mariah—it's Knight, and he's unharmed!"

At first, others argued—"It's just smoke," "No, it's a fence post"—until the shape resolved into muscle and motion, a mane glinting white in the sun. A ripple of disbelief passed through the gathered staff before it gave way to shouts of joy.

Mariah ran toward him, tears cutting streaks down her ash-stained face. Knight lifted his head in the sun and began his trot toward her.

They met in the Sweet Grass pasture. Mariah buried her arms in his neck; Knight pressed back, solid, gentle.

His coat was warm from the fire's radiance, his breath a steady cloud against her cheek.

Around them the other horses pressed near the fence, restless yet oddly quiet, as though they too had been waiting for this reunion. Mariah whispered his name over and over, each syllable a prayer answered.

As they clung together, Mariah's thoughts drifted back to the day she first found him…

Flashback – Knight of Dreams

It was six years ago in Southern California, just weeks after she had received her Doctor of Chiropractic Medicine degree from Palmer College. She was starting her own practice when one of her patients from Santa Barbara told her a story. The woman, Mary Ann, had purchased a horse as a birthday gift for her husband.

Her husband often complained that their large Santa Barbara ranch was empty of animals and filled with weeds. Mary Ann thought the horse would please him. Since he was a large man, she bought a draft horse—a big white gelded Percheron she had found for sale.

Mariah immediately fell in love with the horse. The seller was eager to be rid of the burden of feeding him.

Mary Ann brought the horse home as a surprise. Her husband was indeed surprised—angrily so. "What the hell were you thinking?" he shouted.

The gift became another excuse for his verbal abuse, which soon turned on the horse as well.

Mary Ann was desperate. Mariah had always wanted a horse of her own, and so she bought the Percheron. The papers gave him no name.

"I can't just call you 'Horse,'" Mariah told him. Over time, she felt their minds could meld, their bond a kind of telepathic harmony. She sensed the name he wanted: *Knight.*

"You will be called Knight," she said softly, "and because you answered my dreams, I will name you Knight of Dreams."

Mariah remembered the Santa Barbara ranch as if it were yesterday—wide paddocks of dry earth littered with rusted fence posts, weeds tangling through abandoned troughs. The air smelled of neglect: dust, manure, and disuse. When she led Knight away for the first time, his hooves struck the ground with a hollow finality, as if he too knew he was leaving a place that had never been a home.

That was the beginning of her sanctuary—United in Light—to save horses from slaughter.

Since then, she had rescued hundreds of Draft Horses. Now, she cared for twenty senior, elderly, and abused draft horses.

She usually received the horses when they were over twenty-five, and they lived until they died of old age, often reaching thirty years. Final years of no work, enriching food, and open pastures. Most of all, love—from the staff, from the other horses, and from the multitude of visitors who came to see them and groom them with tenderness.

There was Moon Shadow, a blind Belgian mare whose ribs had shown stark through her hide until months of care restored her to health. There was Freedom, a scarred Shire gelding once used for illegal pulling contests, who now grazed peacefully with the herd. And Old Malcolm, a Clydesdale who had known nothing but the darkness of a slaughterhouse pen until the day Mariah loaded him into her trailer and whispered that he was safe.

All except Promise, her Molly Belle's Premarin foal.

Mariah was pulled from her memories by the cheers of the staff. Knight was safe. The barn could be rebuilt. But in that moment, they knew: their work was more than science. It was sacred.

Scene 2 — Afternoon: Son of White Man Runs Him

Firefighters picked through the ruins. Their chief, Bob Nordloft, lifted a charred beam, sniffed it, studied the pattern of collapse.

"Blast from outside," he said. "I'd call this sabotage."

Mariah exhaled sharply. "Who would do this? And why?"

Son the Director of Operations stood silent. His stillness carried weight.

He was the grandson of White Man Runs Him, the Crow scout who had guided Custer to the Little Bighorn—and lived to tell it. His father had passed down the stories: of a boy who had run from the white man's world, yet carried the white man in his blood. A man who wore feather and army coat, not out of loyalty, but survival.

Mariah glanced at Son, noticing how his expression hardly shifted, but his jaw tightened ever so slightly. In his stillness there was an old gravity, as if generations spoke through the set of his shoulders. The staff nearby sensed it too; they gave him space, watching for what he might say.

Son had chosen another path—veterinary medicine at Purdue—but when he returned to Montana, he felt restless.

Until that day, five years ago, when a vision found him.

High on the 9,295-foot Livingston Peak, overlooking Paradise Valley, Montana, he had dozed in exhaustion from the climb.

In his dream, his grandfather sat by a dying fire, sharpening a broken bayonet.

"Some men speak with feathers. Some with coats. But words are just seeds. Plant them." The old man tossed him a pouch of curled sweet grass seeds.

"Older than horse. Older than flag. They will remember what your blood forgets."

Son woke with the scent of sage in his nose and a clarity he had never known. He hiked down and walked straight to Mariah's ranch. He hadn't left since.

That vision returned now, unbidden, as he stared into the smoking ruins. He felt again the grit of stone beneath his palms on the peak, the fire's dying glow, the pouch of seeds pressing into his hand. It was not only memory—it was instruction.

Now, standing beside the ashes, the same clarity returned.

Scene 3 — Evening: Son Investigates the Destruction

The barn ruins still smoldered when Son returned alone. He knelt where the blast had struck, pulling on gloves to protect his hands from the glowing coals.

"There has to be some evidence here," he murmured.

Searching through the ashes, he found the remnants of an arrow shaft, an empty cardboard dynamite casing bound with chicken gut, and a length of burnt fuse string. He slipped them carefully into a small pouch.

The objects smelled of sulfur and oil, and faintly of blood. Whoever had shot the arrow had handled explosives before—he recognized the rough wrapping technique, the careless scorch marks on the casing. This was no amateur prank.

He traced the arrow's likely path, following the fence line toward the highway.

As he walked the line, the horses lined the fence, watching in silence. When he strayed from the line, they grew restless, nickering and shifting until he returned. In their own way, they were guiding him.

Their eyes glowed from within, heads turning as one to track the unseen line of danger. Son felt a shiver: the Sweet Grass was changing them, sharpening instincts into something more deliberate.

Across the road, in the sagebrush, he found evidence: a patch of flattened stalks, a kneeling impression in the dirt, a scrap of denim torn and bloodstained caught on the sage. He returned to the Ranch house, he had found evidence.

Back at the ranch house, he laid the cloth on Mariah's desk.

"DNA might tell us who fired the arrow," he said.

Mariah's jaw tightened. "And the barn?"

"We'll rebuild it in two weeks."

He looked out the window, toward the labs across the bridge where the grass trials shimmered in the wind.

Seneca Ranch was no longer just horses, or just research. It was both— and it was growing.

They would need more hands. More science.

Son's hand lingered on the pouch of evidence. Whoever had done this hadn't just attacked a barn. They had declared war on Seneca Ranch.

CHAPTER 12

Destroyers After Plan B
Next Day – Morning

Recap: Loss and resolve sharpen as the ranch finds its footing after the blaze.

Scene 1 — Pete's Reaction

Jake drove back into the cabin, still wearing his cowboy disguise. Dust, torn denim, and the stink of sagebrush clung to him.

He thought he had scared the woman at Seneca Ranch, but Pete's network already knew the job had failed.

Failure meant exposure, and exposure meant death. Their contract came with a brutal clause: if exposure threatened W&W's operations, the satellite dish and encrypted gear in the cabin would be destroyed, leaving them stranded—alive, but worthless.

Pete sat in the dim operations room, fury in his eyes. The cabin reeked of sweat and smoke; their submarine rule—nobody bathed, so nobody noticed the body odor—made the air sour. Their props and costumes lay scattered across the floor: cowboys, drifters, hunters. One battered Stetson still bore a faint line of dried blood across the brim, and beside it lay a set of forged ranch ID's the lamination still smelling of plastic and chemicals.

Jake tried to slip past.

Pete snapped. "Don't you walk away from me! You botched it!"

"You didn't brief me right," Jake shot back. "You set me up!"

The fight erupted fast—Jake slamming Pete to the floor, Pete clawing his way back with wiry speed. They grappled like feral dogs until both collapsed, panting. At one point Jake's hand crushed against Pete's throat, choking him. Pete retaliated by picking up a paper weight and with all his might, a sudden smash to Jake's shoulder—a reminder that neither man cared about rules when rage took over.

The crypto alarm cut the silence.

A message glowed: "Report immediately on what went wrong. OUT."

Pete heard the disconnect while wiping blood from his mouth. "Jake, listen. We don't have retirement money. We need this."

Jake's voice cracked. "I know. I thought I could handle it. But the woman and her staff are tougher than we thought—committed. And I should never have gone solo." For a split second, he had a vision of a woman's face flashing in his mind—her eyes steady, unafraid, even when the dynamite went off. He hated how the vision made his gut twist. Pete eyed the torn jeans. "Where's the missing cloth?"

Jake shook his head. "Left it in the sage. No time."

Pete cursed under his breath. "Then let's pray it doesn't come back to us."

He straightened, grim. "Plan C. Same Indigenous theme, but bigger. More aggressive. More men."

He typed an email to W&W asking for more men.

The reply came minutes later, sharp and cold: "STAND BY."

Scene 2 — W&W Virtual Company – Later That Morning

Sam and Hal appeared on split screens, secure video shimmering.

"What a couple of screwups," Sam muttered.

"Idiots," Hal agreed.

"And now they want reinforcements? That's not how this works."

Sam leaned forward. "Still—they've always delivered. Something's different this time."

"They want three more men for Plan C. I'm not cutting into our profits to cover their incompetence." Hal scowled.

"We'll make the client pay."

Sam sighed. "Fine. Call Andre."

Sam's screen showed him in a sterile, corporate office—white walls, blinds drawn, a clock with no numbers ticking softly behind him. Hal's background was darker: a cavernous warehouse with rows of unmarked crates stacked high, lit by a single overhead bulb. Both men looked like ghosts in their own settings, as if the company existed only through their cold voices and faint digital shimmer.

Scene 3 — Hal and Andre's Call

The Quebec slaughterhouse roared in the background when Andre finally picked up.

Hal didn't waste words. "You lied. Ranch size, staff, access. You owe €2,500 in expenses. Pay now. And Plan C will cost €300,000 more."

Andre balked. "Impossible. I must consult my partners." "NO," Hal snapped. "You pay, or you lose everything."

Sweating, Andre tried shifting blame. "My spies say that your contractors failed with the dynamite arrow. Useless."

Hal's voice turned to steel. "Don't test us Andre."

Andre pressed on. "Then let your contractors fix it. Make the Destroyers hire the men and pay from their own fee. They'll have incentive to finish."

Andre winced as the squeal of a panicked horse echoed behind him, the metallic clang of slaughterhouse doors slamming shut. A drop of blood spattered onto the cuff of his white shirt, and he dabbed at it nervously with a tissue, voice trembling.

Hal knew what Sam would say: "Take the money we've got and wash our hands."

Hal commanded, "Andre, if you want to save the money, you call the Destroyers and tell them that you and they have to find the extra men. Leave us out of the negotiations.

"Fine." Andre said to Hal. "What is the number?"

"Here is the number: 1-(899)-606-4573."

Andre said, "Oui." But Hal was no longer on the line.

CHAPTER 13

Destroyers and Andre Connect
Same Day – Afternoon

Recap: Allies gather, but unseen hands push against every fragile gain.

Scene 1 — Cheri

Andre slumped in his office chair, staring at Cheri. She dabbed her eyes, still raw from overhearing Hal's insults.

"Oh, Andre," she whispered in French. "What trouble have you dragged us into?"

She was more than just his assistant—lover, confidante, distraction. Everyone in the office knew about their affair, but none dared mention it.

The staff endured the slaughterhouse stench. Andre and Cheri opened the window to let in the odor. The smell gave an animalistic edge to their lovemaking.

Today, though, Andre asked only for her discretion. "Buy me a prepaid phone. No ID."

She hesitated. "Burner phones? Like criminals use?"

"Just do it, Cheri. It's survival."

She obeyed and left for the phone store.

Andre rose from his chair and leaned against the windowsill, breathing deep as the slaughterhouse odor flooded in. To him it was the smell of money. To his staff, it was the stench of blood and fecal waste. When they heard the window creak, the staff reached into their desk drawers, pulled out absorbent masks, and covered their noses and mouths. The pungent air seeped onto their tongues until they could almost taste the iron of blood. At times the nausea made them gag, but the pay was above average, and a steady job—even in hell—was tolerable.

Andre thought again about Cheri's words: *Andre, what trouble have you dragged us into?*

He liked the *us* in her statement. In his marriage to Shirley, the number of words they had spoken to one another wouldn't fill a single yellow legal pad—and *us* had never once been uttered in their house.

Andre was the pillar of commercialization in his small Quebec town. As the largest employer, his slaughterhouse sustained the grocery store, the feed store, the gas station—every family's survival was linked to him.

He admitted he had gotten too aggressive over the woman in Big Timber. But this was survival time—for him, at least. Other EL'SEC members clung to the status quo. He, however, saw himself as a savior, someone who would drag them into a future they didn't yet recognize.

He imagined his statue in front of the town hall—Andre Laurent, Benefactor. The reality was a line of coughing workers with bloodstained boots, shuffling home through the stench. The only monument to his empire was the endless smoke of the incinerator and the rusting trucks that rattled through town.

Then maybe he and Cheri would escape, leaving these ungrateful people to run the place into the ground.

He laughed at the image and muttered to the empty room, "Let fat Shirley show what she can do without television."

But his thoughts snapped back to reality. The funds he had committed were heavy, dangerous. His dream was pinned to one fragile hope: *EL'SEC would come through. They have to come through.*

Scene 2 — The Call

When Cheri returned with the burner phone, Andre dialed the number Hal had given him.

Pete answered in his flat, no-nonsense voice. "Yes. Make it short."

Andre's tone was clipped, cold. "Your boss says you must recruit the extra men yourselves. And pay them from your own fee. Don't fail again."

The line went dead.

Pete stared at the phone.

Jake muttered, "So it's on us now."

"I don't like this, Jake. A contracted job like this usually runs smooth. But now? Finances, logistics—everything's unraveling. Right now, I think we're in the clear. But if we move ahead with Plan C, there's a real chance we'll get caught. And once they tie us to the other jobs we've pulled, we'll be spending the rest of our lives in prison."

Pete's jaw tightened. He was already irritated with Jake—Jake was the one who botched Plan B. Besides, Pete could use the fifty grand, even if it would shrink with paying three more men.

Jake's voice was small, uncertain. "Then what do we do if we don't take off?"

Pete's eyes hardened. "We find the men. We implement Plan C. And we finish this project—our way."

Pete leaned over the scarred cabin table, pulling a folded map from beneath a pile of disguises. Seneca Ranch was circled in red ink, jagged and heavy, as if carved with a knife. Beside it, a list of names was scribbled—local drifters, ex-military, men who could vanish without a trace. He tapped the paper with a calloused finger, his voice low and final.

"We hire unknowns who don't care if they ever come back."

CHAPTER 14

New York City
Edgar Allan Poe Condo – JP and Mandi Discuss
Barn Bombing
Days Later, Evening

Recap: Secrets surface, pulling JP and Mandi deeper into the currents of danger.

After a quiet weekend in Anacortes, Mandi and I had gone our separate ways. I stopped in California to work with my veteran colleagues at our AI Module near UCLA. We were digging deeper into Premarin, and after my visit I found myself comparing horse communication to whale communication.

Mandi returned to New York to resume her role as President of James-Bandai's Veterinary Division.

On the evening of my arrival in New York, Mandi had finished a long day at headquarters and walked the Hudson pedestrian path to our condo on Edgar Allan Poe Street.

Five years ago, we had found a penthouse condo on Edgar Allan Poe Street—technically an extension of 84th Street. In 1980, New York City officially renamed that block Edgar Allan Poe Street, recognizing Poe's brief residence there during 1844–45. It is believed that Poe drafted parts of *The Raven* during his stay.

James Pharmaceutical headquarters sat just a mile away on the banks of the Hudson River. We often walked to work along the Riverside Park paths, only a block to the west. From our condo deck, we could watch the sun setting over the Hudson River and New Jersey Palisades.

To the east of our condo was Central Park and the site of Tavern on the Green, a restaurant styled after the heyday of New York's roaring 1920s.

In her loneliness of waiting for me, Mandi thought back to our first meeting at a corporate dinner in Tavern on the Green—the night we discovered we were in love.

Flashback

As she sipped her wine, the thought pulled her back five years—to first dinner at Tavern on the Green, where love had first taken root.

Flashback – Tavern on the Green, Five Years Ago

The chandeliers of the Crystal Room shimmered above polished glass and candlelight, scattering reflections across the windows that looked out into Central Park. Outside, the night was alive with the blur of carriages and the muted glow of lamplight along the Mall. Inside, the air carried the murmur of conversation, silver on china, and the faint strains of a jazz trio drifting from the far corner.

JP adjusted his tie, half listening to the board members from James Pharmaceutical, but his eyes kept finding Mandi across the table. She was laughing politely at some executive's story, her hands folded around the stem of her glass, but when she glanced back at him, her smile lingered a heartbeat too long.

The meeting's agenda had been routine—market forecasts, regulatory updates—but here, beneath Tavern's chandeliers, something shifted. For the first time, business slipped quietly into the background.

"Beautiful place," she said later, when they stepped to the tall windows.

JP nodded. "Almost too beautiful for corporate talk."

Their reflections mingled in the glass, Manhattan behind them, Central Park breathing just beyond the panes. And in that stillness, unspoken words filled the space between them—an understanding that the bond they had was no longer defined by strategy decks or quarterly projections.

It was love. Neither of them said it aloud that night, but both knew it. The memory of Tavern's chandeliers would always mark the moment their lives began to entwine.

The jazz trio shifted into a slow ballad, and for a moment the whole room seemed to fade away. Later, JP would remember only the music and Mandi's smile, and the way New York outside the glass felt like the beginning of their story.

Back in the reality of today, Mandi poured herself a glass of chardonnay, set out cheeses, and streamed a Tony Bennett album.

She heard the rumblings of the ancient elevator arrive and the soft beep of our condo keypad.

Smiling, she ducked behind the door, ready to ambush JP.

"Mandi?" I called, stepping inside.

Hands covered my eyes from behind. "Guess who?"

"Jennifer? Deborah? Or maybe… Mandi—with a hint of hand cream?"

Laughing, she leapt into my arms. I carried her straight to the bedroom.

Later, while stretched out on the couch, Mandi asked, "Dinner?"

"I'm hungry," I replied, "but not for cooking—or crowds."

She grinned. "How about Edgar Allan Poe Catering?"

"Should I expect a haunted entrée?"

"Only delicious ones."

As she placed the order, I mixed myself a Grey Goose on the rocks with a dash of olive juice. My favorite, a dirty martini.

I sat down beside Mandi for a restful second, and her phone rang.

She frowned—we had an agreement, phones were always silenced when we were in the condo.

"It's Mariah," she said, already answering. "She wants the call on speaker."

Mariah's voice came fast, anxious: "We were bombed."

"What?" we shouted together.

"Someone fired an arrow with a stick of dynamite strapped to its shaft. The arrow struck the barn and exploded, completely destroying Knight of Dreams' barn. At first we feared Knight had been killed in the explosion, but we found him in a distant pasture—calmly grazing Sweet Grass. He's safe. The barn's gone, but no injuries. Son and the staff contained the fire."

"Why?" Mandi demanded.

"We don't know yet," Mariah said. "But it feels like the start of something. I'll send you a report. You don't need to rush here today, but maybe next week?"

"We'll make plans," Mandi promised. "We love you." And she ended the call. Silence hung between us.

"This is bigger than her letter hinted—bigger than we imagined," I said.

"Much bigger," she agreed. Mandi pressed her hands to her mouth, eyes flashing with both relief and dread. "Thank God Knight's safe… but this isn't just vandalism. It's war."

"We need to be there soon. Not wait until next week."

"Tomorrow," I replied in a commanding, final-decision voice. Then, softer: "But tonight—dinner first."

She smirked, her question left hanging. "And after dinner?"

The doorbell rang—our haunted catering service had arrived. I kissed her deeply before answering.

"What was that for?" she asked.

"Just reminding you that I love you. Now, let's eat—before you invent a headache and we miss dessert."

CHAPTER 15

James-Bandai & DPC Pharmaceuticals, New York City

Recap: Across oceans, EL'SEC maneuvers as rivals close in.

Scene 1 — EL'SEC Conference Call

The next morning, **Georg Messenger**, President of Danube Pharmaceuticals (DPC), sat in a small conference room at James-Bandai Pharmaceutical Company's Manhattan headquarters.

Months earlier, Georg had proposed a partnership with President Phillip Bradshaw—James- Bandai Pharmaceutical CO, strong in the U.S. and Asia, and DPC, dominant in Europe.

Together, they could command global influence.

But before lunch with Phillip, Georg joined an early video call with EL'SEC.

Andre appeared first on the video screen.

For fifteen minutes, he launched into a rampage of warnings about Montana—secretive research, draft horses, and Premarin threats.

He withheld from the Board critical facts: his back-channel deal with W&W as well as the funds he had already committed but did not have and his dependence on EL'SEC to refund his funds.

Jacques cut him short.

"Andre, you exaggerate. We've blocked government interference before. Horse slaughterhouses are still open in Canada. Exports to China are rising. Even synthetic estrogen is losing ground. There is no urgent crisis."

Andre bristled.

"You're blind, Jacques. Clients pay us to act before it's too late."

The other members of the Board shook their heads. Emile advised caution.

Mr. Dwayne Jardine, speaking from Hong Kong, was blunt and gave the PRC standard answer: "In China, we do not steer opinions. We survive them. A disturbance risks dominoes—bad dominoes. I vote no action. Watch and wait."

Georg called for the vote. Every member except Andre voted *yes*. The meeting ended with a sharp click and the screen went dark.

Alone, Georg leaned back uneasily. Twice now Andre had been denied. Yet he persisted, much to the irritation of Georg and the Board members. Andre's obsession had a dangerous edge— one that could either ruin him, or worse, expose something larger that none of them wanted revealed.

Scene 2 — Andre's Reaction

After the call, Andre stared at the blank screen. Relief mixed with fury.

He hadn't secured approval, but he had planted a seed in the Board's mind. Later, he could claim foresight.

Jacques's rebuke stung. He and Jacques had grown up together in French Canada—brothers- in-arms of a sort. Jacques had returned to France, building influence in horse-meat cuisine.

Andre had stayed in Quebec.

For some reason, Jacques did not see the connection: draft horse → slaughterhouse → Paris restaurant tables.

Andre admitted they were divided now. He could not count on Jacques for support. He was on his own.

Cheri slipped into his office and closed the door.

She read the tension on his face. She didn't ask questions, only pressed close.

He smiled faintly, but his thoughts were elsewhere. The fight wasn't over. Not by a long shot.

"Cheri, as much as I would like you to sit on my lap and ease my worries, I am faced with a disastrous situation with my business. I must think."

"Mon âme," Cheri whispered. "You know you have me."

"I know," he replied, holding her off.

She stepped back, trying not to show offense. Hand on the door, she said softly, "Then I guess you don't need me."

"Cheri, please understand—"

But she was already gone.

A staff member, under his breath, but loud enough for the nearby staff to hear, He muttered, "Well, that was short." The staff bent their heads, hiding their smiles at Andre and Cheri's awkward exchange.

Scene 3 — Georg Meets JP and Mandi

At noon, Georg arrived in Phillip's office.

A working lunch had been laid out.

The merger talk was cordial—until Phillip's assistant interrupted.

"Ms. Haynes and Dr. Kornig are here. They say it is urgent."

Mandi and I entered. Phillip made introductions.

Mandi wasted no time.

"We need clearance for immediate travel to my sister's ranch in Montana. An arrow bomb destroyed a barn. The horses are safe, but the research is in danger."

I added, "We also need to advance work on the Sweet Grass alkaloid compound and the James–Seneca Ranch research contract. They're having trouble stabilizing the production process. In its present form, the seed's unstable condition could convert the feed into poison."

At the mention of Seneca Ranch, Georg shot to his feet. His chair toppled. He muttered an apology and recovered, but the reaction was unmistakable. He had tipped his hand—perhaps he knew more than he should about Montana.

Everyone turned when the chair clattered to the floor. Georg forced a chuckle.

"Sorry. Your story about a barn bombing startled me."

We pressed on. After discussion, Georg agreed to remain in the U.S. a few more days. With Phillip's permission, he would accompany us to Montana—framing it as due diligence for a potential research investment.

But inside, Georg wrestled with the truth. Curiosity drew him forward— he needed to see what was happening at Seneca Ranch with his own eyes. At the same time, fear coiled in his chest. If he knew too much, or if Andre's warnings had substance, exposure could bringing ruin not only to Andre but to himself and DPC.

Scene 4 — Planning Montana

Georg confirmed his delay with his Vienna office. His staff didn't fully understand how Montana fit into the merger plans, but it wasn't their place to question.

Phillip approved Georg's travel, arranging for him to join JP and Mandi on the flight to Bozeman International Airport—nearly a hundred miles from Seneca Ranch, but the closest option.

Phillip offered a limo ride to Teterboro Airport the next morning, where JP's Cessna now with it's landing wheels exposed was waiting. I called Teterboro, filed a flight plan, and asked for a maintenance check.

Mandi phoned Mariah to prepare for our visit. Mariah reported that the sheriff had no new leads on the bombing. She welcomed Georg's presence.

That night, Mandi and I soaked in the hot tub, then moved to our bed without breaking our embrace—a ritual since our first night together.

In the steaming water, we spoke about our trip to Montana and why Georg wanted to go along.

"JP, perhaps Georg is simply interested in animal health. Or he just wants to see Montana," Mandi said. "I wouldn't make it a big deal. It might even help the merger. I researched DPC's animal health line—it complements ours."

"Yes," I agreed. "I reviewed Georg's CV. He's smart. Our strategies may complement each other."

Tomorrow would bring Montana, danger, and perhaps the turning of the tide.

Far away, in his Canadian office, Andre lit a cigarette and stared out into the night. The glow of the ember reflected in his eyes as he whispered to himself, "If they won't act, then I will."

The smoke curled upward, like a signal of the trouble already on its way.

CHAPTER 16

South of Great Falls

Recap: New strategies unfold, but the stakes rise with every choice.

The cabin sat back from the county road, half-swallowed by lodgepole pine and wind-bent sage. South of Great Falls the land opened and closed like a fist—coulees, draws, a strip of river flashing pewter between cottonwoods. From the highway it looked empty. Inside, the air was coffee-bitter and hot with anger.

A topo map of Sweet Grass County lay spread across the table. Red grease-pencil rings marked **Seneca Ranch**, **Knight's Barn**, and a handful of gravel turnouts.

Next to the map sat a stapled printout of a Purdue preprint—highlighted, underlined, dog-eared—and a stack of distributor invoices from feed-additive companies with the totals blacked out.

Pete didn't sit. He stood over the table, jaw flexing, a tendon leaping in his cheek every time he breathed.

"They're furious," he said. "W&W is done being patient."

Across from him, Jake kept his eyes on the map. He didn't touch his coffee. "They'll get their result."

"They wanted a horse dead," Pete snapped. "Not a damned bonfire and a headline. You promised it would be inside."

Jake said, each word careful. "Timing shifted. Wind turned. I adjusted, but—"

"But you missed," Pete cut in. His voice cracked like a whip. "And now I have to take the call.

'Explain the deviation. Explain the exposure. Explain why Plan B didn't deliver.' You hear me? Not a barn. The horse."

Silence fell. Only the stove's thin tick and the far-off sound of a freight horn threaded the cabin. Jake finally looked up. "I received some feedback that the Corporate Plan A is still doing what they are supposed to do. Scare the woman."

Pete's laugh was dry and sharp. "Cheap theater."

"Effective theater," Jake countered. "You seeded it. I kept it alive. Corporate read that Purdue article—the cognition markers, the behavioral shift—and they panicked. They could see their billion-dollar market crashing before the ink dried. So they reached for a pawn. Paid some bitter salesman with a bow and a drinking habit to scatter notes through the pasture. That's Plan A."

Pete's lip curled. "And W&W?"
"They watched," Jake said simply. "They saw corporate spooking themselves, and it fit our purpose. Why kill momentum? Arrows at dawn, whispers in the grass—it keeps Seneca jumpy, keeps their research unsteady. Meanwhile, it costs us nothing."

Pete leaned on the table, knuckle tapping the circle at Seneca. "So the pawn gets drunk, brags in a bar, maybe slips a name. Sheriff scoops him up. What then?"

"Then he's a dead end," Jake said. "Disposable. Money chain runs through consulting stipends and prepaid cards. No trace to corporate, and sure as hell no trace to us."

Pete reached for the Purdue preprint and thumbed a highlighted passage. "This is what spooked them. A plant that makes horses smarter, steadier. Promise compound. You don't need a regulator to tell you what that does to the feed industry." He dropped the pages back on the table. "Fine. Plan A keeps running. But it doesn't buy off W&W's temper."

He turned to the window. The glass was scored white where grit had ridden the wind. "W&W wanted proof of reach. They wanted to know we could take a horse out clean."

Jake spoke softer. "We will."

Pete spun back. "No. We won't rerun failure and call it strategy. Plan B is over. Plan C is on deck."

Jake's boots came down from the table. "We don't have the design."

"We have the decision," Pete said flatly. "Destruction. Not splinters and ash for the local paper—**systems**. We take away what keeps the research breathing. Not today, not loud, and not traceable. And not by the two of us playing carpenter with dynamite."

Jake absorbed it, then set his jaw. "W&W signs off?"

"They will," Pete said. "I'll take the call tonight. They'll bark. They'll threaten to replace us. Then they'll remember no one else knows the ground like we do."

A gust shouldered the cabin, rattling the fly strip over the sink. Somewhere in the trees a magpie rattled its dry laugh.

Pete dragged his palm across the table, straightening papers he'd already squared. "Write it down clean," he ordered. "Plan A: intimidation by proxy—corporate funded, continue. Plan B: targeted removal—failed. Plan C: destruction—approved; design pending."
Jake printed the lines in block letters, underlined each, and shut the notebook.

Pete tapped the last line with two fingers. "No improvisation. Not one ounce. W&W wants a result that doesn't bleed back on their shoes."

Jake slid the notebook into a canvas bag. "Arrows for pawns," he said, almost to himself.

"Fires for professionals," Pete finished.

They listened to the wind push at the pines, the freight horn far away, the faint tick of the stove going still. Then they stepped out into the cold and pulled the door tight behind them, leaving the map and its red rings to the shadow.

CHAPTER 17

Big Timber, Montana

Recap: An uneasy calm hides the sharp edge of betrayal.

Scene 1 — Next Morning: Seneca Research Program

Mariah rose at 5:00 a.m. to begin her ranch chores. The acrid scent of smoke still hung faintly in the air, a reminder of the barn fire. Though no one—horse or human—had been harmed, the memory lingered.

She walked to the far end of a Seneca Ranch pasture, Mariah stood in her worn working boots, hands shoved into the back pockets of her jeans. The wind moved across the Montana plains with a steady hush, flattening her hair against her cheek, tugging at the brim of her hat. She remembered one of her first experiences with Sweet Grass. Her eyes had moved to a patch of grass that rippled differently from the rest.

The blades were taller, their hue a darker green laced with silvery edges, as though kissed by a light no other grass received. In the spring sun they swayed with a strange rhythm—soft, strange, almost intentional. And even from where she now stood, Mariah caught the faintest fragrance drifting in the air: a vanilla-like sweetness. Not pungent, not cloying, but soft and unmistakable, a note that lingered just long enough to make her turn her head and breathe it in again.

Promise, her yearling foal, had found it first. He nosed into the patch eagerly, muzzle brushing through the long stems as though seeking something he alone understood. When he chewed, the air lifted with that same delicate odor—subtle, yet so distinct that Mariah felt as though the foal were exhaling a song she hadn't heard before.

Seneca Ranch had been her lifework, built from rescued horses that others deemed broken or useless. Pregnant Premarin mares discarded by the Premarin Farms, carriage horses from city streets, draft teams too old to pull wagons—she took them in, gave them open fields, gave them dignity.

There were mornings when she wondered if she had traded everything else—marriage, children, a simpler life—for this herd. But then she would stand at the fence and watch Knight of Dreams, the old white Percheron who had become the ranch's guardian, raise his head to the dawn, and she knew the choice had never truly been a choice. It was a calling.

Son of White Man Runs Him met her at the stables, where the horses—except for Promise— were already in the pastures, grazing. They rotated pastures systematically, allowing Sweet Grass to regenerate. After a pasture was grazed down, it was replanted with a new hybrid seed, engineered in their lab to yield a stronger variety containing elevated levels of the alkaloid they'd named the *Promise Compound.*

Pelipa, Director of the Research Department, joined them. A poised and striking Zuni woman, Pelipa was born in a pueblo along the Zuni River in New Mexico. She had defied hardship to earn a DVM from the University of Arizona, graduating with honors.

Though her dream had been to serve her people, she found little support for veterinary science back home. Her fortunes changed when Son contacted her with an offer to join the Seneca Ranch project. Skeptical but intrigued, she researched him and learned of his lineage— descendant of a renowned Crow scout from the Custer era. Her upbringing cautioned against trusting outsiders, especially other tribes, but his sincerity had won her over. Three years ago, she moved to Montana to help develop the Sweet Grass hybrid.

That morning, as Son and Mariah stood beside the long, open-air stables, Mariah sensed how serious Son and Pelipa had become. The attack had changed them. Encouraging their closeness, she welcomed the stability it might bring.

"Mariah," Son asked, "when are you heading to Bozeman to meet your sister and the others?"

"Soon. After our pasture walk. I'll stop by the sheriff's office, then pick them up. Mandi, of course, you know. She's bringing her partner JP and Georg Messenger, president of a pharmaceutical company in Vienna."

"Why so many visitors?" Son asked.

"Honestly, I'm not sure. JP may be here to analyze the attacks—he's known for that. But it may also be about the research. As you know, James-Bandai holds the rights to any resulting products."

She turned to Pelipa. "Please prep the lab in case they want a tour."

They began walking. Promise fell into step beside Mariah, brushing her lightly with his shoulder. She stroked his neck in their shared, silent language—taps and slides, like a Morse code of touch. Today, his message was simple: "*Happiness is walking with you.*"

At the newest five-acre pasture, Sweet Grass swayed two feet tall, its vanilla scent thick in the air.

Pelipa inspected the stalks. "No insect damage. The hybrid's resistance is holding."

Promise bolted through the pasture, playfully racing the elder draft horses. His behavior showed no decline. Five years since being fed the first hybrid, he remained healthy—and unusually communicative.

Halfway through their circuit, Son stumbled. Beneath the grass lay an arrow. He yanked it free—its shaft looking somewhat identical to the fragments from the explosive arrow that destroyed Knight's Barn. A note was wrapped around the shaft.

"Don't touch the paper," Mariah cautioned.

Gloved, Son unwrapped it. The words read:

"*Yet… kitái'kó'pohpa?*" — *Are you afraid yet?*

Mariah frowned. "Fresh. Probably shot early this morning."

Pelipa's face hardened as the meaning sank in. "Another arrow?"

She looked from Son to Mariah. "You knew. You've known."

Mariah froze. Son bowed his head, shame in his eyes.

"You let me live here, work here, and never told me?" Pelipa's voice cracked. "I left my people to help you, and you still treat me like an outsider."

Promise reared and backed off at the sudden tension.

Mariah whispered, "You haven't told her?"

Son said nothing. His silence was an admission. Fear flickered in Promise's eyes. For the first time, Son felt it too—not just fear of the attacks, but fear that Pelipa might leave.

Scene 2 — Same Day, Late Morning: Another Arrow

Still holding the shaft, Son sighed. "I should have told her. I didn't want to add to the fear."

Pelipa's eyes were wet, but her voice steady. "You mean this isn't the first?"

Mariah nodded. "There have been several. Notes, arrows, then the barn explosion."

Son added quietly, "We don't think it's the same people. The arrows feel like intimidation— sloppy, meant to rattle us. The dynamite arrow? That was professional. Precise. Two groups, two motives."

Pelipa frowned. "Who would send arrows?"

Son hesitated, then said it aloud: "The feed-additive companies. They read the Purdue paper. They know if Sweet Grass replaces their products, they lose everything. One of them likely paid some washed-up rep to play archer."

Mariah nodded slowly. "And someone—saw the chaos and escalated our war with explosives."

Pelipa shivered. "So we're being squeezed from both ends."

Son rolled the note back onto the shaft. "We'll give it to the sheriff. But we have to assume they're watching us. Our schedule. Our pastures."

Promise exhaled softly, brushing Mariah's shoulder again. His eyes carried the same message as before, only sharper now: *"We're not alone."*ß

Scene 3 — The Sheriff's Office

At noon, Mariah stopped at the Sweet Grass County Sheriff's Office before heading to Bozeman.

Sheriff Tommy Thompson spread photographs across his desk—fragments of arrows, enhanced scans of shafts. "We sent them to the state lab. No prints. But we do have a suspect for the pasture arrows."

Mariah leaned forward.

"Owner of the Road Kill Grill found a man sleeping on her porch. Semi-regular drunk. Dresses like a corporate type who fell on hard times. He rambled last night about 'getting screwed by his horse-feed company'—and about bows and arrows. We brought him in. He admitted firing arrows with notes. But he swears he had nothing to do with the dynamite arrow."

"So the arrows were corporate intimidation," Mariah murmured.

Tommy nodded. "Fits. Cheap stock shafts, easy to source. But the barn arrow? That was handcrafted, precise. Someone wanted to kill, not just scare. Two actors, Mariah. Not one."

She sat back. "That matches our suspicion. Whoever's behind this doesn't just want the horses—they want the research shut down."

Tommy's voice hardened. "Mariah, you're sitting on something big. That grass, those compounds—you're stirring forces that don't like disruption. This isn't just about threats anymore. It's about survival."

Mariah met his gaze, her jaw tight. She understood. The science was no longer discovery. It had become defense.

Chapter 18

Ranch Visitors
Big Timber, Montana

Recap: Conversations twist into confrontations, shaping alliances that may not hold.

Scene 1 — Afternoon, Same Day: Drive from Bozeman to Big Timber

Mariah waited at the private terminal of Bozeman-Yellowstone International Airport until JP's Cessna touched down at noon.

Mandi spotted her sister from the window, waved, then rushed into her arms the moment the stairs lowered.

"I'm so sorry you've had to go through all this," Mandi said. "The terrorism, the threats... I'm glad we're here now."

"Where's the rest of your crew?" Mariah asked.

"JP and Georg are shutting down the Cessna. We'll need to stop before the ranch—Georg is still dressed for Manhattan."

Mariah laughed. "Then Murdoch's first. It's our top western store."

JP and Georg joined them. "Please call me JP," he said warmly. "Mandi's told me a lot about you. I admire what you're doing with the Draft Horses."

Georg inclined his head, smiling. "A pleasure. And yes, I'm aware I'm overdressed for Montana."

"Then Murdoch's it is," Mariah replied.

At Murdoch's, Georg bought Levi's, two pairs of boots, shirts, and a cowboy hat. JP mirrored the order with his own flair.

Their next stop was Ted Turner's restaurant downtown. They slid into a booth at the historic **Baxter Hotel**, where Ted's was located.

"Why does the menu say bison instead of buffalo?" JP asked.

"Because what we have here are American Bison," Mandi explained. "Early settlers called them buffalo, but true buffalo are from Africa and Asia. Ted Turner's correct—these are bison."

Each ordered a bison burger, and by the time the plates were cleared, Mariah leaned in.

"New development this morning. We found another arrow—this one read: *Are you afraid yet?*"

"Did they catch who did it?" Mandi asked.

"The sheriff arrested a drunk bragging about getting paid to shoot arrows into the pasture. He admitted to those, but denied the dynamite arrow."

"Maybe it's over," Georg said.

"I had hoped that this was the case," Mariah replied, "but I am afraid not. Talking to Son this morning, he pointed out some inconsistencies between the pasture arrows and the attack on Knight's Barn. A second theory is emerging—that feed-additive corporations might be behind the arrows.

Sweet Grass as a feed additive could put them out of business."

Her voice darkened. "Until I heard that, I was ready to give a victory speech and say we could finally focus on research. But no such luck."

On the drive east on I-90 from Bozeman to Big Timber, everyone grew quiet, lost in their own thoughts. The green folds of the Gallatin Valley gave way to rolling grasslands.

As the signs for Big Timber appeared, Mariah turned onto Boulder Road. "Welcome to downtown Big Timber. Blink and you'll miss it," she said.

They passed the **Grand Hotel**, its red-brick façade standing proud on McLeod Street.

"That's the Grand," Mariah said. "Built in 1890 when the Northern Pacific Railroad came through. In its day it hosted cattle barons, sheep kings, even railroad executives. During Prohibition it had its share of quiet backroom deals. Now it's our town's pride—a reminder that Big Timber has always been a crossroads, even if a small one."

Next came the Road Kill Grill, and finally the log arch marking Seneca Ranch and Knight of Dreams Road. Mariah turned left onto Knight of Dreams Road.

Draft Horses lined both sides of the road like soldiers.

Georg shook his head. "What a sight."

"They're welcoming me home," Mariah said with a smile.

The breeze shifted, carrying the sweet vanilla fragrance of the Sweet Grass.

"What a fragrance," JP said.

"Sweet Grass," Mariah replied. "You'll see."

Scene 2 — Afternoon: Seneca Ranch

Promise, the tall black gelding with the white mane, trotted alongside the fence as Mariah's ranch truck pulled in the driveway.

He tossed his head toward her.

"He knows you're back," Mandi said. She had seen this before. "He always does."

They were greeted near the stable by Pelipa, Director of Research, and Son, Director of Ranch Operations.

Pelipa extended her hand. "Welcome to Seneca Ranch."

Georg smiled. "The pleasure's ours. I've heard impressive things about what you've done with the Sweet Grass research."

Pelipa's Story

She hadn't been recruited by job posting or phone call. Instead, a pouch of dried Sweet Grass tied with horsehair had arrived in a box, with a note from Son: *"Some medicines are not made to be harvested alone. Visit us in Big Timber."*

She was a recent PhD graduate in Biochemistry, restless in New Mexico, and she came.

When she first walked the pastures, Son paused beside her and said simply, "You were listening."

Her reply: "Since the first blade of Sweet Grass."

And the work began.

Back in the present, Mariah introduced Son and Pelipa to Mandi, JP, and Georg.

"Everything okay since this morning?" she asked.

"All quiet," Son said. "The horses have been grazing peacefully."

"Let's begin with a tour," Mariah suggested to her visitors.

Promise followed them along the fence. When Mariah tapped two fingers on his neck, he lowered his head and breathed into her chest.

"That's his way of saying welcome," she said.

As they walked, Georg asked about the vanilla fragrance.

Mariah explained. "The fragrance comes from the alkaloid coumarin— we've isolated it and now call it the *"Promise Alkaloid"*. We believe it enhances equine cognition and emotional expression."

"And Promise was born to a mare that was fed with the early variant?"

"Exactly. He's our case study. There are behavioral signs," Son added, "but also measurable electrodermal activity—microcharges—when he interacts with Mariah."

Pelipa nodded. "We've adapted wearable sensors to measure it in real time."

Georg looked around the pasture. "Extraordinary."

As the sun dipped behind the hills, they crossed the river and reached the lab. The building rose from the pasture edge, cedar-sided with broad windows that caught the last light. Its clean lines felt both modern and rooted in the land, like a barn reimagined for science. Beyond the glass, faint silhouettes of equipment glowed under sterile light.

The scent of Sweet Grass hung in the air. Tomorrow, the real work would begin.

CHAPTER 19

Son and JP in the Pastures Seneca Ranch – Big Timber, MT
Morning – Next Day

Recap: In boardrooms and barns alike, the balance begins to tilt.

I woke early to the crisp light of a Montana morning. The breeze drifting through the open window stirred the edge of the curtain, and I glanced at the clock: 5:30 AM. The ranch wouldn't be stirring for another half hour, at least.

Mandi was still asleep, having stayed up late with Mariah, their sister talk extending well into the night. I decided to let her rest.

Quietly, I dressed, splashed water on my face, and headed to the kitchen. It was empty. I made myself a cup of Starbucks Breakfast Blend and stepped out the front door.

The ranch was quiet. I walked toward the stables, hoping to spend a bit of time with the horses. As I neared the pasture, I felt a presence. Turning, I saw Son approaching at a brisk pace.

"Good morning, JP," he said. "Sleep well?"

"You bet. Cool mountain air, early sun—what's not to love?"

"Are you out to see the horses?"

"That's the plan. I figured we could do the lab tour later."

"Fair enough. Want to wake Georg?"

"I'd rather observe and think things through on my own first. Let Georg draw his own conclusions." I paused, then added: "You look worried. Are you thinking about ranch access?"

"Yes." Son's tone grew cautious. "When the Boulder River's full, it's boat-friendly. And no, we don't have much security on the river."

He explained how Boulder River's flow over the upstream Natural Bridge depended on water levels—high, and water spilled visibly over a ledge. When the flow dropped, the river vanished underground and reemerged further downstream. This morning, the flow was loud and fast.

"Nature is both shield and weakness," Son said, scanning the horizon. "Water hides as easily as it reveals."

We reached the stables. Several older horses, in their thirties, lay in the hay. I remembered the old saying that horses shouldn't lie down.

"That's a myth," Son corrected gently. "Healthy horses lie down to rest or even enter deep sleep. These old guys likely grazed during the cool night and came back in to rest."

The open stables allowed them to come and go as they pleased. The stalls were oversized, filled with clean hay. We leaned over the stable wall beside an old dark brown Percheron.

"That's Malcolm," Son said. "Thirty-two. Rescued from slaughter. Mariah found him on an Internet listing. He was abused, sent to a feedlot. His next stop would've been a slaughterhouse."

Son's voice turned heavy. "Slaughterhouses don't kill with mercy. Horses are stabbed repeatedly with puntilla knives to paralyze them before being hoisted and cut apart—often still conscious."

"That's... horrific," I said.

"The USDA reports that ninety-two percent of horses sent to slaughter are healthy. Mariah and United In Light have saved hundreds. We try to give them rest after years of hauling plows, carriages, sleds—and sometimes living abused lives."

Son's jaw tightened. "And then there's the Premarin horse."

I frowned. "The medication?"

"Yes," replied Son. "Premarin was approved in 1942—made from pregnant mare urine. That's what the name means—Pre-mar-in. Estrogen is harvested from draft mares kept in narrow stalls, hooked to collection machines almost the entire eleven months of pregnancy."

My stomach tightened. I remembered my mother's struggle with menopause—and the tablets her doctor had given her.

"When the foal is born, it's shipped to slaughter," Son continued, eyes fixed on Malcolm. "Sold for dog food. When the mares are no longer productive, they're fattened for slaughter.
Slaughter is outlawed here, but Canada and China still run the slaughterhouses. The slaughter pipeline never really stops."

Malcolm shifted, as if hearing his story retold.

"That's why Mariah built this place," Son said. "Why we fight. These horses deserve more than a feedlot and a slaughterhouse."

Just then, Promise trotted into the stables. His white blaze stood out against his shiny black coat.

He approached Son and gently pressed his forehead into Son's chest. Son wrapped his arms around him. With one hand, he traced distinct finger movements across Promise's neck. After a moment, Promise lifted his head and gave Son a playful nudge.

Son turned. "JP, meet Promise. Promise, this is Dr. Jean Paul Kornig."

Promise looked at me and stepped forward.

Son instructed, "Duck under his head and hug him. Press into his chest. Clear your mind."

Promise was gigantic. He towered by a head over me. I followed Son's guidance.

As I hugged Promise, something shifted. It wasn't just warmth—it was acknowledgment. I tried to blank my thoughts, but Promise's presence was overwhelming.

A tickle on my right hand distracted me briefly, but I ignored it.

Malcolm rose from his hay and watched us quietly. I could swear… he was smiling.

I stepped back, disoriented. Son, Promise, and Malcolm remained still, almost reverent.

"How do you feel?" Son asked.

"Fine," I said, masking my unease. It was unsettling to feel such equality with a horse.

"Don't be embarrassed. Even we never called horses our equals—only partners. But what's happening here is… new."

Son and I walked into the pasture. I asked about my finger gestures and Promise's response.

"That's what Sweet Grass Hybrid is all about. Over five years, we've seen horses become more sensitive—especially around the neck."

He explained their discovery: "Younger horses, fed Sweet Grass, have shown leadership and emotional intelligence not seen before. Horses communicating—not with sound, but sensation and energy. Their brains may be small compared to the size of the Draft Horse, but what if they've simply been underused or misunderstood? Think about computing—micro doesn't mean less capable."

I nodded. The analogy landed.

"But what about the communication between humans and horses. I have seen you and Mariah communicating with Promise." I asked.

Son stopped, causing me to stop so Son could answer my question. "Over time we have learned a sort of morse code. between the horse and ourself. Promise's Sweet Grass enhanced brain sends electronic pulses. The tingling on his neck that you felt were the pulses. We have worked with Promise and other horses to establish a simple code of basic feelings. As an example, three brain signals from the horse means I am okay or I am feeling good. It is a signal of wellness.

"If the human responds by three taps in response, it means I am okay as well. You can imagine how long it takes to establish a language. But, it is possible. The great thing is, once you train a horse the language between the horse and human, the horse passes the language on to the other horses. You don't have to train all the horses, just one. We have worked mainly with Promise."

"Have there been side effects?" I asked.

"Yes, but nothing serious."

"JP, Mariah told me you had deep experience with alkaloid research. We thought you might be able to help us."

"I'm looking forward to reviewing the research and seeing what I can do."

We both laughed, easing the intensity. Even Promise joined, nickering with what looked like joy. Ten other horses approached, curious and friendly.

Son smiled. "This wasn't a setup for our request for help. But Mandi and Mariah knew you'd want to experience the research firsthand."

"You'll be able to talk to Pelipa, our Director of Research, at lunch and during the lab tour. She'll explain more."

We continued walking. The horses greeted us like old friends. Each nudge and glance felt intentional.

I noticed another group near the ranch house: Mariah, Mandi, Georg, and a woman I didn't recognize.

"Who's that?" I asked.

"That's Pelipa, our Director of Research," Son replied, pride in his voice. "She's given Mariah's vision a language science can understand."

I looked across the pasture, already sensing there was more to this woman—and this work— than I had imagined.

And yet a chill stirred within me. Breakthroughs like this never lived in peace for long. Discovery always drew allies—but it also attracted enemies.

CHAPTER 20

Cabin South – Great Falls, MT

Recap: While the ranch regroups, Pete and Jake lay plans in the shadows.

Scene 1 — Same Day: Peter and Jake Plan an Attack on Seneca Ran

While Georg and JP were being briefed at Seneca Ranch, Pete and Jake were planning their next move, Plan "C."

They had contacted three additional men to join their effort and arranged to meet that evening in a remote cabin to finalize the operation.

To avoid drawing attention, they selected a secluded spot near Great Falls—Judith Cabin Lookout, located off a loop road near the Judith River. The location offered both discretion and a strategic position on the route south to Big Timber.

Pete and Jake arrived in the morning. Their recruits—John, Ron, and Don—showed up later in a fisherman's van, which was intended to transport them along the Boulder River during the operation. Because of the cabin's remoteness, all vehicles were parked down the road at a designated campsite.

The cabin was rustic, a two-story log structure marked as the Judith River Station of the Lewis and Clark National Forest. Pete and Jake greeted the recruits on the porch.

"Welcome to our one-night abode," Pete said. "I'm Pete, and this is my buddy Jake."

The first man stepped forward. "I'm John."

"Ron," said the second.

"And I'm Don," the third said gruffly.

Jake chuckled. "John, Ron, and Don—sounds like a comedy act."

Don scowled. "We're not here to be friends. Names don't matter. I assume even you two don't use real names."

"Fair enough," Pete said.

Don got straight to the point. "Let's talk money first. Before anything happens, we settle up."

Jake nodded. "Pete, pay the men."

Each recruit received $2,500. Afterward, Jake led them inside, where an elk stew dinner awaited in the fully furnished old western-style cabin, complete with floral wallpaper and a wood-burning stove.

"Take your sleeping bags upstairs," Pete said. "Jake and I have the rooms on the left. You three take the right. Dinner's on in ten."

Moments later, a voice yelled from upstairs, "Where the hell's the head?"

Jake called back, laughing, "Try outside, genius. This place is over a hundred years old."

Another voice chimed in, grumbling about outhouses, Sears catalogs, and water hand pumps.

"Only one night," someone muttered.

Soon, all five were seated around the table. Pete sized them up. The trio looked young—early thirties—but hardened by labor and maybe some brushes with the law. Two were whitewater kayaking experts; the third was their driver.

"Who's doing the kayaking?" Pete asked.

"John and Ron," Don said. "I drive."

Pete nodded. "All right, we're here to scare Seneca Ranch into halting their horse research. That's the mission. No killings. Injuries may happen, but we're not getting paid enough to dodge murder charges."

John asked, "What kind of research are they doing?"

"Irrelevant," Pete snapped. "Let's stay focused."

He continued, "The ranch is on alert. Jake blew up a barn using a dynamite-tipped arrow. We also heard of someone else firing arrows onto the property. We don't know who, but it might complicate things."

Pete turned to Don. "Please go over your river plan."

"John and Ron will explain the river action plan," Don said. "I'll drop them in below Natural Bridge State Park and pick them up downriver near the Old Boulder Road."

Ron took over. "We're expert kayakers. We've competed in Class V rapids. We'll launch under cover of night, armed with bows and shafts tipped with dynamite sticks aimed at the research buildings."

"The risk of casualties is low," Ron added.

Jake asked, "Do you know the ranch layout?"

"No," Don replied. "That's your job."

Pete sighed. "We tried to get detailed maps online and by satellite—no luck. So, we're using a drone."

"You're serious?" John asked.

"Very," Pete said. "We picked up a high-end Airborne A2 FLIR drone with long-range thermal vision. Jake, who's great with video games, will pilot it. We'll fly it tomorrow while you are driving to the drop-off. The drone will capture high-res footage. We will text the footage to you in late afternoon before you make you run."

Jake, surprised by Pete's praise, felt a surge of pride.

"Don't worry," Pete assured the group. "You'll have what you need before you hit the river."

They continued reviewing the details of the plan, debating details and refining logistics. After dinner—and several beers—they took turns using the outhouse before heading upstairs to sleep.

Spinning in their heads was: *"It was only for one night."*

Tomorrow, the attack on Seneca Ranch would begin.

Scene 2 — Late Afternoon: Implementing Plan "C"

While JP and the others were immersed in solving problems at Seneca Ranch, Pete and Jake were driving south on US-191 toward Big Timber.

Don, John, and Ron in the fishing van had already driven past Big Timber, headed to the planned insertion point downriver from Seneca Ranch.

Pete and Jake turned west onto the I-90 frontage road toward Carney, Montana—a town in name only. Carney was little more than a grain elevator on the Yellowstone River and a long- forgotten Northern Pacific Railroad stop. Pete figured it would be the perfect, secluded spot to launch the drone and gather the intel Don needed.

They set up behind the crumbling elevator. A dirt road stretched out toward distant ranches; traffic was unlikely. The elevator shielded their truck from both the frontage road and the Interstate.

Pete eyed Jake skeptically. "You sure you're good with this?"

Jake smirked. "No prob, bro."

Pete sighed. *Oh God. He's slipping into stupid mode again. Pressure always does this.*
"Jake, this is critical. We can't screw up. W&W expects a clean op, and we're setting up Don's team. If we botch this, the mission fails—and we lose our payday. Are you really ready?"

"I said I got it, Pete. Trust me. Let me get to work."

They unpacked the Airborne A2 FLIR Thermal X4 Directional Vision Feed Long-Range System drone. Jake powered it up, and its spinning rotors stirred up a cloud of dust from the dry Montana soil.

"Get it in the air fast—someone might see that dust!"

"Relax. I've got this," Jake muttered.

The drone lifted smoothly and hovered as Jake guided it through the iPad interface. He activated the preprogrammed flight plan. The drone would head southeast toward the ranch, avoiding a direct route to skirt low foothills. Jake sent the drone on its way.

They watched it disappear over the ridge.

Jake briefly tested the live feed—high-resolution, crystal-clear video of empty terrain flashed on the screen. He turned the screen off to conserve battery life. When the drone reached its southernmost GPS waypoint, the camera would activate for a northbound river reconnaissance pass.

Twenty minutes later, the GPS signal triggered. Jake tapped the screen and the drone camera came alive.

Pete leaned in. "You getting a feed?"

"Yep. Here it comes."

The first images showed the winding river below, surrounded by dense brush and timber. Then structures appeared—first the sprawling ranch house on the left with a deck over the river. A bridge extended across the water, followed by stables on the left and lab buildings on the right.

After the buildings came pastures filled with grazing horses.

Jake asked, "Think that's enough?"

Pete nodded. "Yeah. Rewind it back to the beginning."

"Sure. One sec."

Jake replayed the video feed on his tablet, enhancing details. They ran the pass three times.

Pete opened the drone's measurement tools, calculating building dimensions using altitude and scale ratios.

Pete dictated a memo of instructions for Don:

"Paddling downriver, The kayak will pass a ranch house on the left with a deck hanging over the river. Then some stables on the left. Then a bridge. After that, on the right, one 20x30-foot building, followed by a large single-story building about 40x80 feet."

Jake nodded. "That good enough?"

"Yeah. Send Don the layout, write-up, and images now—just in case they lose signal at the insertion site."

Jake transmitted the summary. The drone returned, both men silent, knowing the pieces were falling into place—and that Plan "C" was about to be launched.

Scene 3 — Evening: Preparation

Don drove Ron and John through Big Timber on US-191, then onto MT-298. Eight miles in, they turned onto Old Boulder Road and found a fishing landing. After scouting the recover site, they resumed toward the insertion point.

It was still early when they reached the launch site. They had hours to kill before the 11:30 PM launch.

They noted that there was a car in the parking lot, but no people.

They grilled bratwursts with Rhinegold mustard, sauerkraut, and German potato salad. One beer each—then water only. They reviewed Jake's notes, updated their laminated river maps, and burned the river shooting route into memory.

At dusk, the two fly fishermen returned to their car and left.

During next few hours they check all their bow and arrow gear and and the kayak. They went over and over the images from the drone run.

Later, Don checked his watch: 11:00 p.m. "Okay, I'm heading to the extraction point. Good luck guys I will see you in approximately 90 minutes."
"

Ron and John suited up in drysuits, readied the kayak, and slid the kayak into the fast running Boulder River. The current kept pulling the kayak into and down the river. They tied the bow line to a tree that lined the shore, they used a slip knot that would release from the tree when jerked.

At 11:50 PM they got into the kayak.

Ron's shouted—"Release!"—the bow line was released and they launched into the current.

Ahead lay the ranch stretch of the Boulder River.

CHAPTER 21

Same Day – Afternoon: Seneca Ranch Lunch

Recap: Attacks escalate, drawing the ranch into a night of chaos and resolve.

Scene 1 — Lunch

After Son and I finished our visit to the stables and pastures it was time for us to join the rest of the group for lunch.

We all gathered on the deck of the ranch house that overlooked the Boulder River. Two picnic tables were pushed together to form one long table. Our group included Mariah, Mandi, Son, Pelipa, Georg, me. We were joined by six members of the research team.

Lunch was light—Tex-Mex salad and iced tea. The setting was picture-perfect Montana: 85 degrees under a deep blue sky, the sound of the river, and a gentle breeze.

Mariah stood. "I'm so glad we could all gather here today. The only one missing is Promise— and I'm sure if he could be here, he would. If the ranch house didn't block the stables, we'd probably see Promise and Knight at the fence, watching us."

She paused, her gaze warm. "You are each invaluable—to this ranch, to our horses, and to me. Today's lunch is more than a meal. I'd like the research team to share the basics of our work so our visitors have a foundation before we tour the labs. Is that all right with everyone?"

Everyone nodded.

The lunch stretched into a lively two-hour discussion. The team walked us through the evolution of the Sweet Grass Project—how they had worked through four hybrid formulas, each refining the last, yet none perfect.

Mariah explained how it wasn't until they began to see a possible side effect that the project stalled.

"Mandi mentioned your background in alkaloids, JP," she said. "We saw an opportunity to discuss our problem with you. Now, with everyone together, we feel it is time to move from isolated insights to collaboration—one that could not only transform our understanding of equine cognition but potentially yield a James-Bandai product."

She concluded: "So. JP, Pelipa, and the research staff, please adjourn to the labs across the river and the rest of us will talk and take in the sun."

Scene 2 — Lab

The labs were modern and well equipped. Pelipa walked us through the research with pride. I scanned her notes and quickly realized: the Promise Alkaloid was unstable and would degrade over time, sometimes becoming toxic.

Pelipa began her explanation:

"JP, here's where we are, in simple terms. We've moved cleanly through the four classic stages of alkaloid research.

> **Stage One — Discovery and Isolation.** This was really Mariah. Her horses led us to the grass. We used ethanol extraction and ran Thin-Layer Chromatography (TLC) and Nuclear Magnetic Resonance Spectroscopy (NMR). What we extracted is definitely a unique alkaloid. Nothing like it in the databases. Mariah, Son, and I named it the Promise Alkaloid.
>
> **Stage Two — Pharmacological Screening.** Both in the horses and mice, we saw behavioral changes—more focus, calmness, and even faster learning in maze trials.

Stage Three — Synthesis and Structure–Activity Relationship (SAR). This refers to the relationship between the chemical structure of a compound and its biological activity. It helps chemists modify molecular structures to improve activity, reduce toxicity, or alter specificity.
Stage Four — Preclinical. We are currently at this point. Dosing, metabolism, behavioral tracking—it's all ongoing. We are also preparing summaries for regulatory pathways."

I asked: "Pelipa, you've developed what could be a marketable product we could call, Sweet Water Grass™ It is a granular feed additive with the key ingredient being the Promise Alkaloid you isolated. True?"

"Yes," she replied, somewhat sorrowfully. "But in Stage Four, we encountered problems. Side effects."

"I do recommend that we ask Mariah to join us for my recommended solution and conclusion." I paused, "Okay."

"Yes, of course." She used her cell phone to call Mariah and invite her to join us. It was about 10 minutes before Mariah joined us.

After Mariah joined us, "JP I wanted you to know that we observed a side effect after a few weeks on our Sweet Grass compound. It has happened twice and was very scary to all of us. The horse started turning in circles. They were done in place and lasted for 5 minutes."

"I understand Mariah and Pelipa. I think I have the reason for your problem and — Solution."

I explained gently: "Alkaloids in granular feed will break down with heat and moisture. The uncoated particles cause erratic absorption—leading to neurotoxicity. In your correct research protocol, you measured what you put in. But, you didn't measure what the horses absorbed."

I opened a sample bin. The granular mix was damp from fog. The research group had also sweetened the granules with molasses to mask the bitter alkaloid.

"Molasses acts like a solvent," I said. "It pulls the alkaloid through too fast—flooding the system. What isn't absorbed degrades into something worse."

Pelipa looked alarmed. "So we're not just underdosing. Over time we're poisoning them?" I nodded. "Inconsistently. That's the danger."

I could tell that Pelipa had taken this personally when it was just the learning process of researching a marketable product.

"Pelipa, you have done a great job and you should be very proud of what you and your staff have achieved." I said in summary.

"Mariah, I have to tell you how proud you have to be of Pelipa and her staff in what they have done.

I went to a blackboard, I drew small uniform micro-pellets. "These are black on the blackboard but they will be green, waxed, time-release pellets the size of pencil tips. Coated, pH- triggered." I paused for effect, "They bypass the stomach, release slowly in the intestine. No early spike. No degradation in the bin. And no molasses needed."

"Bioavailability?" Pelipa asked.

"Stable across 24 hours. And no cognitive crash at the 48-hour mark."

I smiled. "We can call them NeuroPellets."

Everyone was speechless.

Mariah finally spoke: "This isn't just a compound. It is a marketable product and it is It's a relationship between the horse and us. The horses knew it before we did. If the elder horses could respond, they would say the plant made itself known when we were ready to listen."

Everyone broke into a smile and together they shouted:

"This isn't a medicine. It's a language."

Scene 3 — Celebration – Evening at Seneca Ranch

The late light over the Boulder River softened into gold as everyone drifted back to the ranch house deck for a celebration reception and dinner.

Mariah raised her glass of iced tea. "To Promise, to Sweet Water Grass™ our new product, and to every hand and heart here. Today, we didn't just solve a problem. We found the path forward."

Mandi clinked her glass against Mariah's. "To the first of your goals, Mariah — stabilizing the alkaloid. Tonight we celebrate."

Laughter rolled easy, lighter than it had been in weeks.

Son leaned back in his chair, boots propped on the railing, humming an old ranch tune.

Pelipa smiled for the first time all day, already scribbling *NeuroPellets* in her lab notebook like a name she knew would travel far.

As twilight deepened, the group lingered on the deck. The river's steady rush filled the pauses between their voices.

One by one they left for their rooms at the ranch or headed home, until only Georg and I remained.

Georg and I spent the post celebration discussing the merger and the pros and cons of working together. We knew we had to provide Phillip a report on our recommendations and he would have to share it with the Board of James-Bandai and Bandai's President. Our conclusion and recommendation was to go ahead with the merger. Sure there would be some issues but the bottomline was, go ahead.

As midnight approached, Georg stood beside me, his jacket draped over one shoulder. "One goal down," he said quietly. "Now only one remains — stopping the men who want this place destroyed."

I nodded. "Yes. I keep thinking about the latest arrow in the pasture. I believe it was triggered by the feed-additive companies. Once they learn that we have Sweet Water Grass™ as a food additive, they'll be even more angry — and more likely to act. Tonight we celebrate, but tomorrow… may be something else."

We fell silent, both of us gazing at the black water sliding past the deck posts. Neither of us knew then that even as we savored this fragile victory, danger was already racing toward us from upstream.

CHAPTER 22

The Attack on Seneca Ranch

Recap: Aftermath gives way to reckoning—and questions of who can be trusted.

Scene 1 — Same Day, Midnight: River Attack Run

The current seized the kayak as Ron and John charged downriver.

It was exactly midnight. John swung the bow smoothly to port, lining up their straight run past the ranch.

He sat "in the stern", steadying their course. Ron, in the bow, readied the first arrow. He lit the fuse on the dynamite, notched it, and aimed to port toward the ranch house.

Just before release, Ron spotted two figures standing on the deck. He hesitated—he wasn't a killer. Instinctively, he swung starboard and loosed the arrow toward a pasture outbuilding instead.

Bracing his paddle, he steadied the kayak as they closed on the bridge.

John in the stern, lit his first arrow, aimed starboard, and launched it over the bridge toward the riverside lab buildings.

The kayak shot forward, shadows flickering overhead, whitewater splashing off the rocks. The river's pounding echoed like war drums.

Ron was already preparing his second arrow. He lit the fuse, raised the bow—but the kayak jolted violently sideways. They shot under the bridge. The timbers creaked above as if groaning under the weight of the night.

The kayak emerged on the other side of the bridge. The bridge foundations captured the racing waters and caused large waves that almost capsized the kayak.

Ron's heart leapt, the fuse was sputtering dangerously close to his fingers before he could release the arrow. He aimed left towards the stables but with the jolt the arrow snapped wide, spinning away into the dark.

Explosions erupted up and down the valley. Brilliant flashes lit the ranch buildings and trees, throwing the night into sudden silhouette before plunging it back into darkness. Acrid smoke drifted over the river, and from the pastures came the shrieks of terrified horses. A flock of birds, startled from the cottonwoods, scattered into the black sky.

John fired his last arrow, lofting it high, arcing right toward the large laboratory building. For a moment the lab windows glimmered faintly in the distance—then the arrow struck, and smoke swallowed the light.

They didn't wait to see the result. Both men dug in their paddles, sprinting downriver toward the extraction point. Cold spray stung their faces as the current carried them faster, adrenaline pounding their strokes harder with every bend.

Ron shouted over the roar of the river, "What the hell was that jolt before I let my arrow go?"

John shook his head. "Not sure—but I think someone jumped off the bridge. Tried to grab us. I felt a tug on the stern. Whoever it was, they're in the water now."

"If it was a person, they wouldn't have survived the fall, rocks, and cold water."

Behind them, the river's black surface roiled, a fleeting trail of bubbles breaking into the moonlight before vanishing downstream.

Scene 2 — Same Time: Leap of Faith

I looked at my watch. It was just after midnight. Georg and I had been talking and watching the river rush by. We had just stepped away from the deck railing and started walking back toward the ranch house when, suddenly, a streak of fire flashed across the sky—followed by an explosion on the far side of the river.

"What the hell?" we both said at the same time.

Without hesitation, I broke into a run, heading for the bridge to get a clearer view of what was happening.

As I reached the center of the bridge, another explosion rocked the air—this one over my left shoulder, near the horse stalls.

I didn't think. I acted.

Climbing over the bridge railing, I jumped—my only plan being to land on the boat and stop the attack.

But I hit the river hard, just aft of the kayak. I reached out, fingers grabbing and then my hand slipped off the kayak.

Georg could see the boat surging ahead in the current Cold water enveloped me, pulling me under.

The rapids were swift, relentless.

I resurfaced only to be sucked under again. My arms flailed for balance, trying to avoid the continuous battering of my body against submerged rocks. Each strike jarred my bones, white pain flashing through the dark. The river was no longer water but a living thing—icy teeth biting at my chest, claws dragging me deeper. My lungs screamed for air; every gulp pulled in more river than breath.

A large rogue wave slammed me against a boulder. I felt a sharp blow to my head. Vision blurred. Just before darkness overtook me, one thought broke through: *Mandi's face—if this is it, at least I tried.* Then nothing.

Unconscious, my body was carried by the river—I was tossed and turned like a rag doll, bumping from rock to rock in the churning flow.

From the deck, Georg had seen me leap. He had yelled, "Stop, JP!" but it was too late.

He sprinted to the bridge, shouting, "Man overboard!" and peered into the water. But JP was gone.

For an instant, Georg was no longer on a Montana ranch but back in a European trench, the cries of "Man down!" echoing through smoke and fire. His hands gripped the bridge rail so tightly the wood cut into his palms. He forced himself back to the present, but the weight in his chest told him he'd already failed.

More explosions lit the night sky—the arrows striking the large lab building. The explosion sent flaming debris into the old lab down the river.

The fiery bursts illuminated the kayak as it raced downstream. Chaos unfolded around the ranch.

Scene 3 — Midnight: Ranch Chaos

The ranch was in utter chaos.

People were running in every direction—some in bedclothes—trying to shield themselves, others racing to safeguard the horses. No one knew if the attack was finished or if more explosions would follow. Coordination was impossible amid the panic.

Mariah, seeing that most of the explosive arrows had struck near the river buildings, sprinted to the deck and grabbed a powerful megaphone. Her voice rang out sharp and urgent:

"Stop! Everyone stop running. If you're in a safe place, stay there!"

She repeated the message three times before the frantic motion began to slow.

Breathless, she continued, "I think the attack is over. It looks like only the lab buildings were targeted.

Mariah shouted orders:

"First—we need to make sure no one is hurt. If you're injured, or know someone who is, get them to the main ranch house.

"Second—we need to put out the fires at the lab and save as much of our research as we can." "Third—we need to make sure the horses are safe and the pastures are not on fire.

Below, a woman shouted, "The hay barn's on fire!"

Another voice, panicked: "Where's the foaling shed crew? Somebody check the mares!"

The words rippled through the crowd like sparks, but Mariah's steady tone over the megaphone anchored them.

Suddenly a terrified gelding broke free from its halter, eyes rolling white in the firelight. It reared, snapping a post loose, then bolted across the yard. Two wranglers sprinted after it, shouting, while smoke and flames painted their shadows long against the barn walls.

Mandi hurried up onto the deck, joining Mariah. "Is there anything I can do?" she asked.

"Head to the main lab building. Make sure the sprinkler system is on and assess the damage." Mandi nodded and bolted toward the bridge, vanishing into the smoky night.

Across the river, Mariah caught sight of Son running upstream. She raised the megaphone: "Son, where are you going?"

Son skidded to a halt and looked back at her. "To the old lab buildings! I want to make sure the fire doesn't spread to the surrounding brush.

Others seem to be handling the main lab." He hesitated, then called back, "Is that okay?"

"Good move," Mariah answered. "Just don't take unnecessary risks. There might be old fire extinguishers that might explode with the heat."

Beside her, Georg stayed silent, watching as Mariah directed the chaos with crisp authority.

Even through the smoke and confusion, she never wavered. He felt a quiet surge of respect— on this night, it was Mariah who carried the command presence, the voice everyone needed.

Scene 4 — One Hour Past Midnight: Where are Jean Paul and Georg?

Mariah asked anyone who would listen, her voice sharp with urgency: "Has anyone seen Georg or JP—the two men who were with me this afternoon?"

Pelipa spoke up. "No. But the reason I got to the ranch house so fast after the explosions was that I had been taking a late walk when the first one hit. The noise was so loud, I started running away from the labs, thinking I should get to the other side of the river. I could swear I heard a male voice yell, 'Man overboard!' I didn't think anything of it at the time—everything was in chaos."

Mariah froze. That phrase—*Man overboard*—meant something. It wasn't the kind of cry for help someone floating downstream would usually make. It was a boating term, used when a person fell from a vessel. If one of the attackers had been thrown from the kayak, they would have shouted "Help!" or nothing at all. But both Georg and JP were boaters. Navy men. If one of them had seen the other fall into the water, their training would have triggered that instinctive cry: *Man overboard.*

That had to be it. One of them had gone into the river.

Mariah turned to Kanti, one of the staff members. "Round up some of the staff and start walking downriver along this side. Someone may have jumped in during the explosions and been swept downstream."

"Will do, Mariah," Kanti replied. "I sure hope no one did. That part of the river is dangerous— there are submerged rocks, and the current's swift. It doesn't calm down until well beyond the ranch. If someone made it past the rocks, they might have been washed up at the bend after the meadows. A few of us have floated that stretch in inner tubes—just for fun. We always beach them at the end of the meadow and hike back up to go again."

As Kanti hurried off, Mariah stayed rooted where she stood. She gripped the megaphone tightly, her knuckles pale in the firelight. A hollow dread spread through her chest. *JP... Georg...* The names pressed against her thoughts like a weight she couldn't shake. It was one thing to lose a building, even a lab filled with months of work. But to lose either of them— especially JP—was unthinkable. The river had already taken too many lives in Montana. She prayed silently that it wouldn't claim another tonight.

Scene 5 — Boulder River 30 Minutes Later

When Georg saw JP go over the bridge railing and then the kayak emerge from the other side of the bridge without him, he knew JP was in the river, heading downstream.

Without hesitation, Georg left the deck and sprinted along the riverbank, scanning for any sign of his new friend.

Moonlight lit his path, but the river was treacherous. The current surged over boulders, throwing up whitecaps, and in the dim light, it was hard to distinguish a bobbing head from a rock.

Georg reminded himself: *rocks don't move—heads do.* Every time he spotted something that might be JP, he froze, watching intently. So far, everything had remained still. His worry deepened.

JP could be hung up somewhere along the shore, hidden by brush, Georg thought.

He recalled from earlier—while standing on the deck—that the river calmed just beyond the lab buildings. After that came a bend to the left and wide gravel and sand bars on either side. He'd noted before that anything drifting downriver without control often washed up on those bars. If JP had any strength left, that's where he'd end up.

Georg stayed on the ranch house side of the river until he reached the calmer section— nothing. He realized he'd need to cross over to check the opposite shore. That meant doubling back to the bridge, costing him precious minutes.

He raced back and across the bridge, casting a brief glance at the chaos engulfing the ranch— flames licking the lab buildings, shouts echoing, panicked horses tearing at their lead ropes, vehicles arriving with sirens wailing. For an instant, the scene pulled at him—every instinct as a leader telling him to stop and help. But then he forced his focus back to the water. *One man's life now. That's my mission.*

Sticking close to the river, Georg passed between the lab buildings and the water. The fire's heat pressed against his skin, making him sweat, but he pushed on. No one paid him any attention—everyone was absorbed in their desperate tasks.

By the time the blazes seemed mostly under control, Georg had reached the sand bar. Then a cloud swallowed the moon, plunging everything into blackness. He stopped, heart pounding, straining his eyes toward the debris-littered shore. Driftwood of every shape and size piled high across the beach. In the dark, it was impossible to tell if a body might be hidden among it.

Finally, the moon broke free again. Shadows sharpened. Georg resumed his search, methodical, weaving among the logs and scanning every angle. Just as the beach tapered off, he spotted a shape—longer, smoother than driftwood, but ambiguous in the pale light. It could still be a log.

Georg sprinted toward it, stumbling twice—once over a thick root, again as his foot slipped in loose gravel. He dropped to his knees beside the shape.

It was a body.

It was JP.

And he wasn't moving.

Georg's throat caught. "JP… God, no." His hand shook as he touched JP's shoulder, half afraid the body would be cold. "Stay with me, brother. You're not done yet."

Scene 6 — Just After the Raid: JP is Down

The first thing I realized—I was alive. Cold water wrapped around me like iron bands, dragging me downstream. My lungs burned, each breath tasting of river grit and smoke. I had no idea how long I'd been unconscious or how far I'd drifted.

How stupid was it to jump off that bridge? The thought hammered through the fog. No chance of hitting the kayak. No chance at all. Now the only plan left was survival.

I tested my arms. Pain flared white-hot in the shoulders, then dulled into numbness. The cold was working in my favor—masking damage I didn't want to know about. I tried a kick. No pain. My legs obeyed. Good. I raised my head to look—light stabbed behind my eyes—but through the haze I glimpsed a bend in the river, a pale smear of gravel beach. Hope.

I fought to keep myself angled that way, kicking, letting the current do most of the work. My body wanted to roll midstream, to surrender. I refused. Every stroke drained me further.

Knees scraped gravel. I clawed at the riverbed, dragging myself inch by inch out of the current. Water tore at my legs, then shoved me forward like it wanted me gone. Finally I collapsed on the bar, face down in grit and driftwood. Upstream, fire's orange glow painted the sky. *The ranch. I'm close. Someone will come.*

Pain swallowed the thought. Darkness took me again.

Georg dropped to his knees beside the body. JP. Shredded clothes, limp limbs, face half- buried in gravel. He pressed his fingers to the neck—faint pulse. Relief, then dread. The river could wash away blood, but not injuries this deep.

"Stay with me, JP," Georg muttered.

A cough shuddered through JP's chest. His eyes flickered, unfocused. The sound of Georg's voice seemed to tether him back.

"It's okay," Georg said quickly. "You're alive. You're badly hurt. I won't move you."

JP's lips moved, no words—just bubbles of blood and river water. His eyes spoke the rest:

Don't leave me.

Georg scanned quickly, hands ghosting over limbs, checking for bleeding. "I can't see where it's bad. Don't move. Understand?"

More bubbles. A gurgle that almost sounded like *yes.*

"I have to get help," Georg whispered. "Time's not on our side."

No. Don't leave. But JP's voice failed him. Consciousness slipped again.

Georg sprinted back upriver, legs hammering against the gravel. The ranch loomed with firelight and shouts. On the far bank, staff moved with hoses and buckets.

He cupped his hands and shouted, "Yo! I need help!" Instinct carried the words in German first, sharp and clipped. Blank stares answered him. He tried again in English, breath ragged:

"I found Dr. Kornig—downriver! He's alive but critical! I need a litter and plank, now!"

This time people understood. Kanti broke from the group, running full tilt toward the bridge. "How can I help?"

"JP's downriver," Georg gasped. "Broken bones, maybe spinal. He can't move. We immobilize him on a plank, then straight into an Evaluation Emergency Litter. Call for a medivac helo."

"Understood." Kanti spun and sprinted for the ranch house.

Moments later, Mandi and Pelipa emerged from the chaos. Mandi saw Georg's face and knew. She broke into a run.

"Show me," she demanded, grabbing his arm. Together they sprinted to the bend.

JP hadn't moved. His skin was pale, lips bluish in the moonlight. Mandi knelt, hand hovering. Georg caught her wrist.

"Don't. He's fragile. Just let him feel your touch—forehead only." She did, whispering, "JP, I'm here."

Shouts carried across the river. Four people ran toward them with a plank and litter. Georg took command—quick, clipped orders. They dug carefully under JP, slid the plank beneath without twisting his body, and lifted him onto the litter. Every movement drew a groan from JP's unconscious form.

The group carried him swiftly toward the bridge.

Whop-whop-whop. Rotor blades cut the night. Searchlights swept the ranch. The Livingston Trauma helicopter.

Mariah's voice carried from the deck. "They'll have him airborne in ten!"

On the sand bar, Georg and Mandi jogged beside the stretcher team. JP's body jolted with each step. The helicopter's wind tore at their clothes.

And then JP was airborne, Mandi with him. The sound of rotors faded into the night, leaving the ranch smoldering and silent in the aftermath.

CHAPTER 23

Extraction of the Attackers

Recap: In the quiet, strategies sharpen for what must come next.

Scene 1 — Extraction

At 1:00 AM, Don reached the eddy at the river split. Whitewater thundered right, calm current swirled left. He thought the kayak would be there waiting for him. He got out of the fishing van and looked downriver.

Suddenly the kayak burst through the chute, battered but upright.

"Thought you bought it," Don muttered as he hauled John and Ron ashore. Both were shivering, hands scraped raw from the rocks.

Don asked, "How did it go?"

"Right on plan." replied Ron and John in harmony.

Within fifteen minutes, the kayak was broken down, stowed, and the van rolling.

John and Ron stripped off their dry suits and pulled on flannel shirts and fishing caps.

Don kept the headlights off, guiding the van along the rutted dirt road by moonlight towards the city and then home.

Inside the fishing van, John muttered, "Swear I heard someone jump from that bridge. Like they aimed for us. Ron you saw men on the deck which caused you to fire the arrow away from the stables for fear that you might hit the men."

Ron snorted. "Yes I saw them and one was running towards the bridge. It must have been him, Anyway, no way anyone survives that water."

John commented, "Why are the headlights off."

"I can see the road and I thought it would be safer. If we see another car, we can turn them back on."

They laughed, but uneasily.

Scene 2 — Sheriff's Trap

Sheriff Tommy Thompson after hearing the explosion, closed off all roads leading out of the Boulder River area south of the city. His plan was to trap anyone running from the explosion before the could get the the Interstate.

Deputies blocked Route 298; Tommy covered Old Boulder Road.

Then—Tommy saw a dark image coming up the road towards him without headlights. Don, saw the Big Timber Sheriffs car blocking the road.

The same time Tommy saw the dark car coming up the road he turned on his headlights and flashing red light and siren.

Once Tommy saw that the fishing van was going to stop he stepped out, hand resting casually on his holster.

Don stopped.

Tommy walked up to the driver's door window and asked for the drivers "License and registration."

"Will a rental agreement do?" Don replied easily, opening the glove box. "That'll work. But why you were driving without headlights?

Care to explain?" "Moonlight. Thought it'd be nice. Would've turned them on for traffic."

John grinned. "Everything was silvery—by the light of the silvery moon—" "Shut it," Tommy barked.

Tommy ordered them out, collected IDs—false, but tidy. He swept the van's interior. He stopped. The kayak gleamed in the beam.

"That's enough. Van's impounded. Don—you're in lockup. The other two, open cell. Move."

Scene 3 — Don's Plan

At the jail, Don leaned close to John and Ron's cell and spoke through the bars. Don would stay behind locked bars for driving without headlights. Ron and john in the next cell but the door was a jar.

"Listen. I'm locked up. You're not. Wait till the sheriff goes home. Then get to the van. Dump the kayak, dry suits—everything. Keep the fishing gear. Make it normal. It's our only shot. No evidence no case."

Outside, the river still thundered. Inside, the plan was already in motion.

As dawn's first pale light touched the Crazy Mountains, echoes of the night still lingered— smoke over Seneca Ranch, sirens fading toward Livingston, and the sheriff's trap snapping shut on the fleeing attackers. Yet amid the arrests and evidence, the real battle was just beginning.

A helicopter thundered low across the valley, carrying JP toward the trauma center. His fight for survival was no longer on the riverbank, but under the bright, relentless lights of surgery.

CHAPTER 24

The Livingston Trauma Center
Next Day – Early Morning

Recap: Choices in far-off rooms ripple back to Montana's fields.

Scene 1 — Helicopter

The helicopter descended through a slate-gray sky, its blades chopping the air above Livingston, Montana. Below, floodlights illuminated the trauma center's rooftop pad, casting long, jittering shadows across the surrounding mountains.

It was 3:15 AM when the skids touched down. The rotors thundered, blowing grit against the glass doors as the trauma team rushed forward with a gurney.

Inside the helicopter, JP looked deathly pale beneath the straps. Blood flecked his shirt, his right arm bent unnaturally, lips cracked from the river's cold. His breath rasped shallowly, barely lifting his chest.

Mandi clung to his side until a nurse's hand touched her shoulder.

"You can't come in," the woman shouted over the roar. "We'll keep you informed. Family room, just through those doors."

Mandi hesitated, eyes locked on JP's unmoving face. Then she nodded, trembling, and stepped back.

The gurney vanished into bright light.

Scene 2 — Inside the Trauma Bay

Dr. Lynn Caldwell, Livingston's senior trauma surgeon, snapped on gloves and leaned over the patient.

She had seen dozens of wrecks on these roads—hunters tossed from ATVs, miners crushed under rigs—but something about this man was different. He wasn't just battered; he was broken. And yet his body clung to life with a stubborn pulse, as if refusing permission to quit.

"Vitals," she ordered.

"BP sixty over forty. Oxygenation low. Possible hypothermia." "Cut the clothes. Full assessment."

Scissors hissed. Wet fabric peeled back, revealing livid bruises blooming across JP's ribs and abdomen.

Caldwell's eyes narrowed. The pattern wasn't just blunt trauma—it was river damage. Rocks had slammed him, tossed him, left angry purple crescents along bone.

"Get ultrasound. Rule out internal bleeding."

The probe slid across his abdomen. A breathless pause. "No free fluid." "Good. At least the river hadn't torn his insides apart."

"CT next. Prep for surgery. Fractures are obvious: four ribs, scapula, compound fracture of the humerus."

A junior resident whispered, "He shouldn't be alive." Caldwell ignored her. "He is. Move."

Scene 3 — The Family Room

Mandi sat hunched in a plastic chair, knuckles white around a Styrofoam cup of untouched coffee.

The wall clock ticked, its sound magnified in the sterile quiet.

Every half hour, a liaison nurse appeared with updates. Stable, then unstable, then stabilized again. Surgery imminent.

Mandi's mind raced in circles. She remembered JP on the deck just yesterday morning, teasing her about Montana coffee. His hands had been warm, his smile crooked. Now those same hands were strapped down, punctured with IV lines.

She whispered into the silence: Don't leave me, not now. Not when we've only just begun.

At 6:00 AM, footsteps clicked against tile. Dr. Caldwell entered, shoulders bowed with exhaustion but voice steady.

"He made it so far. The arm is repaired. Bleeding controlled. He's in ICU—stable, but critical. The next forty-eight hours are the real test."

Relief buckled Mandi's knees. She clutched the surgeon's hands, tears streaking her cheeks. "Can I see him?"

"Soon," Caldwell said gently. "He's still under anesthesia."

Scene 4 — At Seneca Ranch

Meanwhile, dawn crept reluctantly across the valley. The air still smelled of smoke and charred cedar.

Mariah had not slept; she hadn't even tried. Her voice was hoarse from barking orders through the night.

Volunteers and ranchers swarmed across the grounds: hauling hoses, clearing debris, hammering boards across shattered windows. The labs still smoldered, but the vaults had held.

At sunrise, state investigators arrived with drone files intercepted from Jake's fly by. Grainy footage, sent anonymously to Mariah's inbox, revealed the full assault in chilling clarity—arrows igniting as they struck, detonations blooming in the night. It was no accident, no prank. It was warfare.

Mariah stood on the deck, mug of black coffee warming her hands. Below her, the pasture lay scarred but alive. Horses stamped nervously in the stalls, their eyes wide, nostrils flaring at the lingering smoke.

"They came for us," she whispered. "And we're still standing. And JP—he's still with us." Her words vanished into the morning haze, carried off by the restless wind.

Scene 5 — ICU

When Mandi was finally allowed in to see JP, she barely recognized him.

JP lay swaddled in white sheets, his body a map of bruises and bandages. Machines hummed steadily, each beep a fragile promise.

She sat in a chair beside his bed, pressing her hand over his.

"I'm here," she whispered, though he could not yet hear. "And I'm not letting go."

Outside the window, sunlight broke over the Absaroka mountains, gilding the snowcaps. The world was scarred, but dawn had returned.

CHAPTER 25

Was This the End of Terrorism?
Seneca Ranch – Morning

Recap: Lines are crossed, and the fight for the horses deepens.

Sheriff Tommy Thompson drove back toward Seneca Ranch, headlights cutting through the smoky dark.

On Route 298 he passed only a few drunks weaving home from the Road Kill Grill. His deputies fell in behind him, weary but alert. He felt sure he had the attackers in custody—but he needed to see Mariah, to hear the whole story himself.

At 4 AM, both patrol cars rolled up Knight of Dreams Road. Volunteers wandered sleeplessly through the yard, their faces streaked with soot, voices hoarse from shouting through the night.

Tommy's deputy moved off to gather statements. Tommy knocked at the ranch house door. Mariah answered, drawn and exhausted, but steady. She let him in.

The great room had become a gathering place. Georg sat with a stack of security stills, Son hunched over a radio, Pelipa scribbled notes on a legal pad. Coffee, smoke, and the faint trace of whiskey lingered together in the air.

"I'm sorry this happened," Tommy said quietly. "But I think we're close to ending it. I stopped three men on Old Boulder Road—fishermen, so they claimed. Their story doesn't add up.

They're locked up now. But I need your account." Everyone began talking at once. Mariah raised a hand.

"Let me tell it," she said. Her voice was raw but firm. "The rest of you can add details."

And so she began—the story that would be remembered as *The Night Seneca Ranch Was Attacked by Terrorists.*

When she finished, Tommy stood, hat in hand. "Oh, I am sorry I forgot to tell you some news that I received today from the Bozeman National Guard Station that has a listening station on Livingston Peak. They keep an electronic listening device that monitors Bozeman, Livingston, and Big Timber.

Every perked up.

Tommy continued, "I have not had a chance to review the tape as I don't have the right equipment. Without the equipment the sound is not very good and the resolution of the video is terrible."

I'll take the tape and all the other evidence I have straight to Helena. If the men and any others found on the tape are part of something bigger, we'll know soon." He tipped his hat, then left her to the silence that followed.

CHAPTER 26

Voices in the Ashes Seneca Ranch – Same Morning

Recap: Even allies must face the cost of what is being defended.

Dawn crept slowly over Seneca Ranch. Smoke hung in the fields; the air carried the scorched tang of chemicals and charred wood. Horses shifted nervously in their stalls. Birds stayed silent.

Mariah stood at the pasture line, arms crossed, watching the pale blue sky fight through the haze. Behind her, the ranch house hummed like a command post—radios crackling, men and women moving with grim purpose, mugs of bitter coffee in every hand.

Inside, Sheriff Thompson sat with a yellow pad full of notes. Georg studied the lab camera feeds, zooming in on shadowed figures.

"What about the Ranch security cameras. Any help?" asked Georg,

Son replied, "For some reason we did not think the river was a threat. We had all cameras on the horses and buildings. JP and I talked about river access this morning. A weak link in security that I will fix. Talk about closing the barn door after the horse has bolted."

Pelipa reported that Mariah hadn't spoken in an hour. "I'll talk to her," Georg said.

He found her rooted in the dirt, boots planted like stone. "You're thinking of leaving," he said gently.

"I'm thinking of giving it all up," she admitted. "The grass, the sanctuary—what's the point, if people are willing to kill to stop us?"

Georg stood beside her. "People once burned libraries to destroy knowledge. The truth still survived. This isn't a war, Mariah—it's a revolution. Revolutions only win when the people carrying the truth refuse to break."

She turned slightly, eyes shining. "When the fire started, Promise looked at me. Not with fear— like he knew. But, like he was telling me something."

"Then maybe now's the time to listen," Georg said.

Back in the house, Son reported grim news: "Two of the men in custody have paramilitary records. One out of South Africa, one from Southeast Asia. Not weekend fishermen. The two of them are now locked up, along with the driver."

"The driver. Always the driver," Pelipa muttered.

Tommy entered with a lighter expression. "We've got federal eyes now on all three. Homeland Security is sending someone this afternoon."

By midday, a black SUV rolled up the gravel road.

A woman stepped out of the official auto—early forties, navy field jacket, dark hair pulled back. She flipped open a leather case: **Special Agent Danielle Vance, Homeland Security.**

"I'm here to assess this incident, classify it, and make sure your research is protected," she said.

Mariah studied her warily. "And if your investigation says we're the threat?"

Vance didn't flinch. Her tone was measured, almost reassuring. "Then we have a different conversation. But until then—we work as a team. That's the only way forward."

Sunlight finally broke through, falling across the pasture. The grass bent softly in the wind, carrying whispers only Mariah seemed to hear.

CHAPTER 27

Cabin South
South of Great Falls – Same Morning

Recap: Pete and Jake wait in the silence of the forest.

The cabin crouched low against the slope, half-hidden by lodgepole pine and talus. From the porch you could see nothing but trees and the pale band of sky. Smoke from the south drifted in long, thin veils—someone else's problem, somewhere else.

Pete stood at the rail with binoculars he didn't need. Habit more than purpose. He listened for what wasn't there—no tires on gravel, no human voices, just a jay heckling the quiet and a breeze combing the needles.

Jake came out with a battered AM radio and set it on the crate they used as a deck table. He tuned past static until the news cut through.

"—three men in custody in connection with the Seneca Ranch explosions. Sheriff Tommy Thompson declined to comment on additional suspects—"

Pete's mouth twitched. "Three. Not five."

"Don's boys," Jake said, lowering himself into a camp chair. He stretched his legs, boots knocking the rifle case by the door. "Means the sheriff still thinks fishermen throw fireworks." Pete poured coffee thick as tar and handed him a tin mug. "Means we keep it that way."

They listened until the update looped, then Jake turned the volume down.

Back in their luxury cabin, Pete tapped his knuckle on the operation table. "If we need to meet the three of them again it's a public cabin. We didn't bring anyone here. So far we don't exist."

Jake snorted. "Don never knew our cabin ever existed. He can sing all day and the choir still won't find us."

Pete didn't smile. "He might sing anyway."

"Let him." Jake rolled the mug between his palms. "They'll ask for names. He'll give them what he heard—Pete and Jake. Which, last I checked, is nobody."

Pete crossed to his chair, opened a flat steel case, and set a thumb drive on the table. Next came a small black hard drive wrapped in oilcloth. He laid them side by side like cards.

"Insurance," he said.

Jake's eyebrows lifted. "You pulled it?"

"Everything the bird saw," Andre said. "Thermal passes, northbound run, the bridge, the buildings, the pasture layout. And the information off the iPAD tablet cache—comms, timestamps, a scrape of the sat-call metadata from our liaison." He put a fingertip on the hard drive. "If anyone decides to get righteous, this buys time."

They viewed the tape.

"Jake," exclaimed Pete. "You taped the actual run?"

"While you were sleeping. Remember we decided to stay put behind the silos until we saw or heard the explosion. Well you fell asleep. I knew the launch of the run was midnight so I sent the drone back to the kayak launch point and filmed the attack run."

"Jake, sometimes you amaze me."

Jake leaned back, chair creaking. "What's the plan —silence or run?" "Whichever we need first."

For a while they said nothing. The radio mumbled road conditions. A squirrel skittered along the roofline. The world outside the trees felt abstract, like a story they'd already heard.

"You think W&W will call?" Jake asked at last.

"They'll wait for a read," Pete said. "W&W likes distance both in time and geographic. They'll wait until their intelligence feedback receives a report" He let the sentence end there.

Pete wrapped the hard drive and thumb drive again, slid them back into the steel case, then into the false bottom of an ammo can. He set the can with two others and stacked a folded tarp on top.

"Two days here," Pete said. "No calls. No roads. Then we drift. Spokane. Or Medicine Hat. We let the juice die."

"And Don's team?" asked Jake.

"Don's already picked his angle," Pete said. "Driver who didn't shoot. Late-night fish. He'll toss names to sweeten the deal. They won't stick. He never saw our plates, never set foot in this cabin."

Jake nodded toward the wallet kit. "We changing skins?" Pete opened the top tray and slid two IDs free.

"Carlson and Brant," he said, as if trying the weight of the words. He passed one across. "Burn the old."

Jake glanced at the laminate—picture, birth date, a signature close enough to his hand if no one looked too hard. He tucked it into his pocket and stood.

They stepped out to the burn aluminum barrel. Jake fed in the remnants: a map corner with a penciled waypoint, an empty fuse tin, two prepaid SIMs clipped in half, then the cheap wallets that had had their false ID's.

Pete struck a match, held it until flame curled the edge of plastic and paper, then dropped them into the barrel. Blue smoke coiled up and disappeared into the brighter morning.

"Anything else?" Jake asked.

"Drone's clean and buried." Pete shrugged. "If they ever find it, it's a catalog model a hundred ranchers buy. Nothing ties to us."

They returned to the cabin. The radio burbled again, this time a caller was speculating about tariffs and foreign currency.

Jake turned off the radio. He broke open a pack of Canadian cigarettes, lit one and took a drag. He paused, listening to the wind blowing through the pines.

"You hear it?" Pete asked.

"What?."

"The quiet. After. Like the world takes a breath."

Pete slid the bolt across the door, half out of habit. "It's the only part I still like."

They sat again, two men in a cabin that might as well not exist. When the wind shifted they could smell the forest fires burning and smoking the area. Jake said, "The night fires, far and faint, like a postcard from something already over".

Jake cleared his throat. "You think the salesman keeps his nerve? Will he disclose the corporations?"

Pete took a long drink and set the cup down. His eyes were hard in the slanted light. "If he doesn't, someone will help him find it."

Jake watched a jay hop along the porch rail and flick into the trees. "You ever get tired of finishing other men's messes?"

Pete didn't answer. He checked his watch and the tree line and the empty road that wasn't there. He'd learned a long time ago that the questions you didn't answer were the ones that kept you breathing.

"Two days," he repeated. "Then we're ghosts again."

They let the cabin be a cabin and the forest be a forest. South of Great Falls, the world held its breath and pretended not to know their names.

After two days with the cabin cleaned, Pete and Jake were gone. Whether they vanished across the border or into the ground was never clear. At Seneca Ranch, no one asked—the silence of outside violence was its own kind of closure.

CHAPTER 28

The Investigation Deepens
Seneca Ranch, Montana

Recap: At Seneca Ranch, the night of fire finally ended. JP was flown to Livingston Trauma, Mariah stood in the ashes, and Sheriff Tommy secured suspects. But questions loomed larger than arrests—the attack reached beyond Montana.

By afternoon the day after the ranch attack the ranch property was crowded with state police, federal agents, and equine regulators. Their vehicles lined the gravel drive in a silent procession of authority.

Mariah, still in smoke-stained clothes, stood near Sheriff Tommy as he briefed the investigators.

Georg Messenger, composed but weary, stepped forward and broke the silence.

"This isn't just a local crime," Georg said. "You should know about EL'SEC—an international oversight body for equine ethics, science, and commerce. I serve as its Chairman."

The officials exchanged glances. Tommy stiffened. Mariah's eyes narrowed.

"Our mandate spans genetic research, pharmaceutical use, and global policy," Georg continued. "We investigate unethical practices—illegal trafficking, misuse of equine products, unauthorized experimentation. What happened here was no random act. It was designed to intimidate and derail ethical progress."

After Georg's unexpected announcement. Everyone was stunned into silence.

The first thought of the group was, "So what does that have to do with the bombing?" "Georg, what are you talking about?" asked Mariah.

"I meant to tell you all earlier but I did not have enough information to tie these terrorist acts to a member of the EL'SEC Board. After yesterday I am 100% sure that a member of my Board was behind this act of terror. I am sure he was not an active participant but his signature is all over the plan."

Mariah's voice was sharp with anger and loss of trust. "Do you think someone inside EL'SEC is involved?"

Georg hesitated for only a moment. "No. But someone may be independently exploiting their position on the Board. In fact the Board supports research on the classification of horses among other issues favorable to horses and humans. The truth will surface when the Board meets. EL'SEC has every reason to defend projects like yours."

One investigator jumped in with legal action on their mind and asked Georg, "Can you share records on EL'SEC?"

"I cannot," Georg replied evenly. "Bylaws forbid it without Board consent. It is a breach of Board ethics. The plan possibly came from an individual acting outside our code of conduct."

Evidence began to mount. Drone parts were traced to a shell company— W&W Risk Management. Financial trails led deeper still, to a European horse-processing conglomerate.

The signatory: Andre Laurent.

Interpol was alerted. Subpoenas issued. Andre's shadow was finally visible.

That evening, Georg briefed select EL'SEC members on a secure call. No names yet, only that a breach threatened a global equine initiative.

Sir Simon Danridge, the reserved British member, spoke: "We must prepare for a formal hearing of the full Board. Until verified, this remains strictly confidential."

Georg nodded. "I'll bring a dossier to Melk. EL'SEC will not ignore this betrayal." Mariah called Mandi to give her an update.

Mandi told Mariah that JP was healing very well and shortly he will be discharged and they would be back at the Ranch.

There was nothing permanent, she reported. Thank God.

Mandi, told Mariah that JP wanted Mariah to know that he was not really surprised at Georg's EL'SEC disclosure. He had talked to Georg… he told Georg he'd join him in Vienna the moment the doctors let him out of this hospital prison.

He followed up his trip remark by having Mandi tell Mariah that he had told Mandi that Georg is a very smart businessman and he is involved with many international activities. I am glad he is on our team. If the person responsible for all of these terror acts is on Georg's Board, I am sure he will take care of the situation.

Mariah had responded to Mandi's report. "Outsiders wanted to destroy our Ranch. Instead, they lit a fire under us."

CHAPTER 29

Shadows over Melk
A Week Later

Recap: With evidence mounting—drone wreckage, financial trails, and Andre's signature—the hunt for accountability left Montana. Georg carried the dossier across the ocean, into the fortress halls of EL'SEC.

The monastery bells tolled over the Danube as the EL'SEC Board assembled in the ancient wine cellar boardroom. The vaulted chamber was quiet, save for the scrape of chairs against stone and the faint echo of centuries pressed into the walls.

Seven members sat around the oak table, their faces half-lit by the dim chandeliers.
Georg Messenger entered with a leather dossier under his arm. The weight of Montana's ashes seemed to follow him inside. He set the dossier on the table, his voice steady but edged with resolve.

He looked around the table. One chair—Andre's—was empty.

"Where is Andre?" Georg asked flatly.

Silence.

Jacques spoke up. "I talked to him by phone. He said he would be here."

Moments later, the boom of the great oak door echoed down the stairwell. Heavy footsteps descended.

"That must be Andre," Jacques murmured.

Andre entered with the flourish of a man expecting applause. He radiated confidence, imagining himself vindicated—believing the Board would now approve his actions and authorize the funds he needed to cover his debts. To his mind, the Montana crisis was solved. Research halted, horses safe as livestock—he expected congratulations, not condemnation.

He sat. No one spoke. Faces were blank, unreadable. Georg said, "Andre, good of you to join us."

Andre smiled thinly. "The train was late." In truth, he had paused for a beer to steel himself, convinced this meeting would end in approval.

Jacques scoffed. "Austrian trains? Late? Ridiculous."

Andre was taken aback at Jacques's statement. He depended on Jacques's support and his ability to influence the Board toward his side of the argument. This was a very strong message that he might be in this situation alone. He looked at Jacques with a guessable stare. Jacques continued to look straight ahead and avoided eye contact.

Andre moved in his chair responding to his loss of what he depended upon to be a strong supporter. He came to a conclusion that he was alone.

Georg banged the gavel once. "This meeting was called because Andre insisted he had urgent business. We asked him to provide proof that there was a conspiracy to reclassify horses as social animals. While we waited for him to arrive, each of you read a report before you that I supplied based on personal experience—detailing the bombing of Seneca Ranch in Montana."

Andre's face changed instantly, the smile erased. He half-rose, protesting. "Monsieur Chairman, what are you talk—"

Georg raised his hand, palm forward. "Sit down, Andre. And be silent."

Georg opened the dossier. Photographs, drone footage, forensic reports spread across the table. Wire transfers traced to W&W Risk Management. At the bottom, a signature: Andre Laurent.

Andre protested. That is privileged data. "I don't even…" he stopped.

Georg finished the sentence for him, "have a copy."

"How" Andre started but Georg finished his sentence, "did I get a copy. It seems like the gang you used to bomb the Seneca Ranch used a drone to do research and then monitor the attack. Unknown by the gang member, there was a National Guard Listening post listening for any transmission over the area and they downloaded a copy which now is being used as evidence against you."

He continued, "It is ironical that the evidence we kept asking you to provide for your urgent request to take action is now being used as evidence against your breach of ethics."

Paper rustled. Eyes sharpened. Andre sat like a stone in the surf.

"It's not true," he muttered. "I was told—"

"Silence," Georg snapped.

Sir Simon Danridge broke the quiet, his tone clipped. "The evidence is serious. It cannot be dismissed. But our bylaws demand a hearing before sanction."

Georg's reply was calm, but iron. "Compensation you want for your actions taken without our sanction? You financed mercenaries. You set fire to sovereign soil. Lives were nearly lost. And you dared to call it defense of our industry?"

The words rang like a bell in the chamber.

Andre's hand clenched. His mask slipped, revealing raw desperation. "Without strong measures on this kind of research, the world will descend into chaos. Governments are weak, regulators slower still. Someone had to act. I acted where this Board hesitated."

Sir Simon cut into Andre's heart. "No. You acted outside the code. And the code is what binds us."

Sally Glasco leaned forward, eyes unwavering. "Mr. Laurent, the shell companies—W&W and its satellites—do not absolve intent. They mask it. And masking is not a defense under our charter. Per Bylaw IV, Section 12, I recommend immediate suspension of Mr. Laurent's voting rights, privileges, and system access."

Georg set his palm on the dossier. "So ordered. The Ethics Committee is hereby convened. The hearing will begin immediately."

He banged the gavel.

Andre sank back, his eyes darting across the table. For the first time, the fortress walls of Melk were not sheltering him—they were closing in.

CHAPTER 30

The Fall of the House of Laurent

Recap: Andre was suspended, dossier evidence sealed under wax. But the Ethics Board was already in session. What began as oversight now sharpened into judgment.

Scene 1 — Melk, Austria – Ethics Hearing

The vaulted doors of the wine cellar closed. Files lay open: bank records, shell accounts, drone stills and videos, forensic reports. Faces around the table were set in hard lines.

Georg stacked the evidence neatly before him.

"Exhibit A: Bank records—W&W payments routed through a shell tied to Andre. Exhibit B: Drone imagery—approach path, impacts, timestamps. Exhibit C: Forensics—identical incendiary residue from van to lab."

Sally Glasco spoke first. "Monsieur Laurent, do you deny authorizing payments to W&W?"

Andre forced a smile. "Logistics vendors are routine in our industry."

Dieter from Germany's gaze did not waver. "Not for arson and armed intrusion. This wasn't freight—it was force."

Andre spread his hands. "Coincidences stitched into a tale."

Georg kept his voice level. "The dossier shows intent and concealment. By bylaws, I recuse from the vote. But I move that the Board consider censure, sanction, and expulsion."

Andre's eyes hardened. "You'd sacrifice a producer to please sentimentalists." "No," Georg said. "To uphold ethics."

The Board conferred briefly. Sally rose. "Under Section 9.4, the Board censures and expels Andre Laurent. Effective immediately."

Andre shoved back his chair. "You protect feelings over food!" Georg's voice cut like steel. "We protect the future over your past." The chamber doors boomed as he stormed out.

Scene 2 — Canada, Next Evening

Andre's journey home was long and bitter. Train to Vienna, flight to Quebec, then a car ride through cold air that smelled of wet steel and slaughter.

At his office at J'aime Les Chevaux complex, the office staff greeted him with applause, oblivious to Andre's situation.

Cherie maintaining a stately secretary decorum rose from her desk chair. She stood ready to greet her boss. She opened his office door for him and started to follow him in to his office for some return home activity. Instead Andre closed the door behind him shutting her out.

Andre, moved quickly to the window and opened it for the slaughterhouse odor.

Cherie would not be shut out. She opened the office door, Shut it after her entrance and rushed to him, arms open. She kissed him, whispering, "Mon amant…you are home."

But when Andre turned around, she drew back, she saw tears streaking his cheeks. "Andre, what is wrong?"

His body shook. He clung to her, sobbing. "They destroyed me. Expelled me. Ten years gone. All gone."

The staff outside, hearing the muffled sounds, mistook them for passion. They smiled—"Andre is back, all is normal."

But Cherie knew better.

She tried to soothe him. "Come, mon amour. Visit the line—it always steadied you." Andre nodded weakly. "Yes. Walk with me."

At the slaughterhouse, he told her softly: "Go back, Cherie. I need to be alone." She hesitated. Then obeyed.

Andre entered the slaughterhouse and walked the catwalk above the moving line. All the workers were on a break and he was alone. The sight of carcasses that once filled him with triumph and represented profit. Now mocked him.

Fury burst. He screamed into the vast halls of the plant: "How could you do this to me!" He just stood there screaming. Something in Andre's mind snapped.

The slaughter room stank of blood and disinfectant. Chains rattled, drains gurgled, and from the hooks overhead the previously killed horse quivered the carcass still dripped blood into the grate. He would kill them all.

Andre moved with a swagger, rolling the puntilla knife between his fingers. The blade was small, almost delicate compared to the captive bolt gun on the table, but he knew its purpose — not death, not clean at least. The puntilla was meant for paralysis, a crude thrust at the base of the neck to drop a horse into silence before the longer sticking knife was drawn. It was a butcher's tool, a bullring relic.

Andre grinned, holding the knife up to the light. "Elegant, isn't it?" he said to no one. The gleam was sharp, cruel. He imagined the thrust, the collapse, the helpless eyes still conscious. Power without mercy.

But in his carelessness he had dragged the blade across a frayed electrical conduit, slicing insulation. The arc cracked, blue and sudden. Sparks leapt into the damp sawdust and pooled blood. For an instant Andre saw the flame chase the floor as though the whole slaughterhouse itself had chosen to answer him back.

A small explosion drowned out his laughter, the puntilla still clutched in his hand as fire consumed steel and flesh alike.

He had tried to escape down the catwalk and out the entrance. But he slipped on the blood- slick steel floor and fell into the chute holding onto the legs of a butchered Draft Horse/

The resulting explosion blew the plant apart.

Cherie was making her way back to the Administration building when the plant blew up. The concussion of the explosion knocked Cherie down and into the bushes that lined the sidewalk.

She lay where she had fallen, shaken, and trying to make some sense of the situation. She felt the heat from the burning building and suddenly remembered that Andre was in the building.

There was no way Andre had made his way out. She sat in the bushes and all of a sudden remembered that with Andre gone, she was free. Free of a nice man but also free of a more than heavy slaughterhouse boss.

Cherie picked herself up, brushed off Andre's favorite skirt and walked to her car in the parking lot. A smile crossed her face as she walked.

She was focused on the car and getting out of this life. She didn't think of anything but her escape plan. She ran into Andre's wife Shirley who was responding to the explosion. In her haste Cherie accidentally knocked Shirley to the ground. Cherie never missed a step.

By afternoon, only twisted beams and ash remained.

In the rubble lay a scorched sign with the name of the building: *J'aime Les Chevaux* — "I love horses."

Far away, at Seneca Ranch, a white draft horse named Knight of Dreams lifted its head as if hearing an echo—then bent again to graze Sweet Water Grass™.

CHAPTER 31

Seneca Ranch Sweet Water Grass™
Two Months Later

Recap: The fires and hearings are behind them. JP healed, Andre fell, and EL'SEC stood firm.
But the real work—science, healing, and new beginnings—has only just begun.

Scene 1 — Future

The morning sun filtered through the high windows of the newly rebuilt Seneca Ranch laboratory. Warm beams of wood and stone gave the space a quiet strength.

Mariah and her sister Mandi stood at the window, watching a pair of Draft Horses graze in the restored meadow where Sweet Water Grass™ now grew in segmented pastures.

Mandi said, "Can you believe just a short while ago we were sifting through numerous bombings and fires."

"I know," replied Mariah. "Now look at us. Rebuilt and growing. More laboratory buildings, more land, and more Draft Horses. And look at Promise still acting as if he is the king of the herd."

Mandi corrected Mariah. "We can't call them a herd any longer, They are a community. A herd is a livestock term." She went on, "And look, there is Knight standing on the far side of the pasture overseeing his community."

They continued to watch the community life unfold before their eyes.

Mandi snapped out of her watching the horses. She was thinking of JP. "Mariah, let's thank the Livingston Hospital for bring JP back to us." One month of surgery and rehab brought JP back to Mandi.

Now JP was in Vienna talking to Georg about merging. His company with James-Bandai. What a powerful Pharmaceutical Company that will be."

"JP was brought back to us," added Mariah. "His work with Pelipa is bringing Sweet Water Grass™ to a marketable product in such a short period of time. What you have done is amazing."

Mandi added. "The feed-additive corporations lost to *Sweet Water Grass*™. JP tells me that they have been hounding him about agreements on joint research projects with United in Light and Purdue University. He tells me at the moment there is no foundation for grant research. This is not a vendetta but just being realistic. They advertised that their look alike products do the same as *Sweet Water Grass*™.

Their products would only add to cost and not benefit. I led them on but they are now beyond the curve of horse feed. Let them go bankrupt trying to beat us. He said let them try and beat Mariah. He summarized with: Ain't progress great?

Mariah cell phone rang. She held the phone to her ear.

"How's the first production run?" JP asked on a call from Vienna.

"Better than I hoped," Mariah said. "The grass holds its cognitive signature even dried and granulated. Tablet formulation shows a 22% improvement in equine memory and calmer behavior."

"And human trials?" asked JP, always looking toward the future.

"Too early yet for human trials," Mariah replied. "We plan to get the horse feed product off the ground and established first. We'll have peer-reviewed data in sixty days."

JP's voice brightened. "Then reclassifying horses as social sentients isn't just a dream. It's proof."

"It's justice," Mariah replied. "I have to go—Son's waving at me. Take care."

Across the room, Son tapped his tablet. "Press requests—Wired, *Nature*, even the local network. They want the story."

"Not yet," Mariah said. "Science first. Licensing secure. Then the world."

Son hesitated, then added quietly, "Sheriff Thompson sent word. The three men in custody took plea deals—reckless endangerment, property damage. Light sentences. What about the two planners known as Pete and Jake?"

"Gone. Vanished into the hills south of Great Falls. No IDs. No trail."

Mariah's jaw tightened. "Then they'll resurface. Men like that always do. Talk to you later" And ended the conversation.

Later her phone buzzed again—JP from Vienna. "You're on speaker," Mariah said.

My voice came through clear: "Philip and I just received Board approval. The James-Bandai merger with DPC moves forward. The name for now: James-Bandai-Danube Therapeutics— JBDT. Sweet Water Grass™ is the new company's flagship product."

Outside, the horses grazed quietly by the river. The same waters that once carried danger now shimmered in peace.

CHAPTER 32

Seneca Ranch
The Vows and the Vision

Recap: With the ranch rebuilt and partnerships reshaped, JP and Mandi turn to each other. From corporate halls to riverbanks, a new venture—and a marriage—begins.

The wedding was simple, as Mandi and I always wished. Beside the Boulder River, with wildflowers on the breeze, fresh lemon odor, and horses grazing nearby.

Mariah performed the Wedding Service, her voice steady, despite tears.

Georg stood beside me as my Best Man. Son, bolo tie shining was an Usher. Pelipa in her Zuni dress was the Maid of Honor.

I met Mandi's eyes. "With you, I found a purpose deeper than patents and profits." She smiled. "With you, I found a partner—in work and in life."

When rings were exchanged, cheers rose. Overhead, two eagles drifted in lazy circles, silent witnesses.

I thought it was my imagination but I swear I could hear the horses stomping their hooves. That evening on the deck, Mandi rested her head on my shoulder.

"So—what do we call our new venture."

"We have a new Venture?" I acted surprised although we had discussed a new venture the day before.

"JP, you know very well what new venture." Mandi said somewhat indignant. "NinthWave Biobotanica?" I offered.

Her smile widened. "Perfect. The next wave."

And so began our independent institute—dedicated to uncovering the medicinal secrets of overlooked plants.

Our first case was to be a herb in Washington State's Olympic Mountains with dermatologic burn advantages. Before we became involved in changing the classification of Draft Horses, I had spoken to the designer of our home in Anacortes, WA."

I went on, "He had told me about a plant that could have burn therapeutic properties. The local tribe had told me that there was a long history with this plant. Mostly in cancer treatment, but other uses were a mystery. When I had heard more of the story I think this plant might change everything we know about battlefield medicine."

CHAPTER 33

Washington, D.C.
Whales, Horses, and Laws

Recap: From ranch fires to boardroom battles, the story reaches the Capitol. The whisper of Sweet Water Grass becomes the roar of policy.

On the Capitol steps, sunlight lit a crowd of advocates and reporters. Senator Diane Calloway stood at the podium.

"Today, we honor an animal that has carried our burdens and healed our souls. With this Act, the United States recognizes the horse not as livestock, but as a social companion species."

Applause thundered. Cameras flashed.

Mandi squeezed my hand. Mariah breathed deeply, eyes closed.

The law now banned slaughter of horses for human consumption, ended exports, and recognized horses as sentient beings. A turning point, modeled after marine mammal protections.

The ceremony was outstanding except for the hecklers in the crowd. We could only assume that these were people that were horse meat eaters. Although when I questioned a few of them, they didn't have any idea what we were talking about and what this legislation means to our animal community. I found out they were paid by an activist and just wanted to protest.

The corporate media jumped at reporting that there were protestors to the government having a legislation to protect horses. One young person told me it was none of the governments business to change horses from livestock to social animals. That final statement made headlines the following day.

That day we learned that the European Union had outlawed any exports of edible horse meat to any countries including the USA. The majority of citizens of the world did not want to eat horses.

Later, under cherry trees on the Washington DC Mall, Georg reported: "EL'SEC has followed the U.S. lead. Andre was expelled. His assets liquidated to cover damages."

Mariah nodded. "And Sweet Water Grass™ now holds protected research status in both the U.S. and EU."

I smiled. "Our venture began with a whisper. Now it's a voice the world can hear."

EPILOGUE

Whispers Still Heard

Montana's plains exhaled green and gold. Horses moved in silence, the Sweet Water Grass™ whispering in the wind.

On an area in a far pasture of Seneca Ranch were the burial grounds of the Draft Horses that United in Light had saved from slaughter and had passed in fields of Sweet Water Grass™ of old age. Each grave stone had a marker stating their name and age. Over the entrance of the sacred ground was an arch with a bronze plaque:

In honor of those who heard the whispers—and answered.

Mariah on a bench in one of the pastures sat thinking of how far she and Promise had come. Behind her, stood Promise now a fully grown Percheron watching over the community. Across the river, researchers prepared for another day's work.

In the restored lab, Pelipa and Son continued their careful stewardship of the Sweet Water Grass™ trials. Mariah trusted them both, their quiet dedication a reminder that the work would outlast the chaos.

In Vienna, Georg ran his division of JBDP. He also worked with the owners of EL'SEC to make this collaborative stronger and ensure that members like Andre never acquired membership.

EL'SEC was rebuilt, expanded its influence on world ethics and was a stronger international organization Mandi and I moved to our home in Anacortes, WA to pursue more challenges in plant life with espionage issues as NinthWave Biobotanica.

And in the stillness, the grass whispered again—not a warning, but a promise.